SING NO SAD SONGS

Chris O'Brien is a happy man. The wise-cracking private-eye is looking forward to a quiet few months, but a trip to London to visit his girlfriend Debra gets him involved in a hunt to find a gang of neo-nazi thugs. Back in Bradford a chance meeting with an old friend is followed by her suicide, and whilst trying to deal with his guilt O'Brien tracks down a psychotherapist whose job it is to heal, and is horrified by what he uncovers. As things escalate O'Brien and Debra assemble a multi-ethnic band of brothers to meet adversity. Adversity is about to get its ass kicked...

SING NO SAD SONGS

SING NO SAD SONGS

by

Christian Thompson

Magna Large Print Books
Long Preston, North Yorkshire,
BD23 4ND, England.

British Library Cataloguing in Publication Data.

Thompson, Christian
    Sing no sad songs.

    A catalogue record of this book is
    available from the British Library

    ISBN   0-7505-2198-8

First published in Great Britain in 2003 by Allison & Busby Ltd.

Published in Large Print 2004 by arrangement with
Allison & Busby Ltd.

Magna Large Print is an imprint of Library Magna Books Ltd.

Printed and bound in Great Britain by
T.J. (International) Ltd., Cornwall, PL28 8RW

To my Sarah.

No one else
Can make me feel
The colours that you bring

Prologue

There was a cigarette end on the floor that had missed the ashtray. That was what she stared at. Not for any reason. But if you stared long enough you could come up with any reasons you wanted. Some you didn't want, too. The mind was like that. She had learned a lot about the mind recently. All of it frightened her.

The ashtray was mounted in a column of black metal the height of all the chair arms. The sturdy, varnished chair arms. There were small burns and rubbed-in grey stains in the carpet around it. The mat-thin fire resistant carpet. The brown carpet.

The beige tab end of the cigarette was bent double in a V shape. She thought to herself that it was like a little person, kneeling or bowing. It wasn't alone either. Another bent the same way. Two more unbent – prostrate in worship. Then she remembered a picture of that place where all the Muslims go to or face towards when they pray. What was it called again? Allah? No. Then she thought of the joke about the Bingo Hall. Mecca. That was it. The ashtray was Mecca.

She almost smiled to herself for coming up with the image. She knew that she'd almost smiled because she felt her dry lips creaking, cracking at the corners, pulling slightly apart where they had stuck together in the middle. She used to be good at making her friends laugh. A long time ago.

She turned to one of the others sitting in the chairs and mumbled, 'That cigarette's a Muslim.'

As soon as she heard herself she regretted it. She sounded like a mad woman. She hardly spoke at all now for fear of saying mad stuff. She didn't mean to. It was just the way it came out.

The man didn't answer anyway. A stream of smoke drifted out of his face, curled around and hung in a layer in the centre of what they called the Day Room. He carried on staring at whatever he was staring at. He wasn't listening. She was glad he wasn't one of the nurses. She didn't think he was anyway.

It had been difficult to tell at first. They weren't like proper nurses. They didn't wear uniforms. They didn't take temperatures. They didn't *bustle*. Some were smart, some were scruffy. Some were kind, some were ignorant. Some smoked straights, some roll-ups. You could say the same about the patients too.

One of the nurses leaned into the day room without entering it. She was very thin, with wispy blonde hair and a nose stud.

'Medication time,' she said to no one in particular.

Then she walked off. Brushing her hair out of her eyes and sniffing loudly as she did so.

Medication. It had helped at first. She had been able to sleep properly for the first time in ages. Not anymore. Now it seemed to slow her down and hold her back. Locked up inside her own body. She couldn't think. She was starting to forget why she was here. She was starting to fear that she might crack up good and proper – start believing some of the lies she had been told.

Before long the nurse came back. She had forgotten to go and queue up. Some nurses would bring her medication to her. Others insisted that everyone stand in a shuffling line in front of a white metal trolley that blocked the clinic room door.

'You can always have your injection if you refuse oral medication,' said the blonde

13

nurse. She said it in an offhand manner that sounded unfeeling but was supposed to cover up the implied threat. Shadows loomed behind her in the doorway.

She panicked at that. She remembered the last time. The humiliation. The burning pain as the fluid pumped in. The stiffness that stayed in her neck and jaw. The unrefreshing cotton wool sleep that followed.

The panic moved her despite herself. She stumbled forward. The only place to run was the corner.

Pathetically, she tried to hide herself. Pulling at a heavy chair to try and move it away from the wall, trying to get behind it.

'Careful, she's going to throw the chair!' she heard one of them say.

Throw it? She could barely shift it.

They grabbed her. She tried very hard not to move – not struggle so that they would let go – but the stiffness of her body must have been interpreted as resistance because they began to walk her away.

'Take her to her bed area,' said one of the men.

Bed area. It was a single bedroom. She didn't know why they called it that.

'We're concerned about your dignity even if you are not, Linzi,' said the blonde girl. It

14

was said in a fairly soft voice so it can't have been intended to sound as insulting as it did.

Fifteen minutes later it was over and she was back in the day room. She felt not sleepy but far away. She would have preferred to stay on her bed but they had insisted on her being out here so they could 'observe' her. Funnily enough, none of them were anywhere to be seen.

She wanted to go to bed now. She didn't want to disturb anyone. She felt vulnerable here. A few days ago a man had touched her leg. The same man was the only other person in the room and he seemed to be leering at her helplessness.

She pushed herself up from the chair awkwardly; unfortunately she knocked over the metal ashtray as she did so.

Shhh! she thought. Don't attract attention. She tried edging along the wall quietly. She misjudged the doorway, fell to her knees, and was beginning to crawl her way up the corridor when the nursing staff reached her.

'She's kicking off!' shouted the leery man gleefully from the day room. He stood and waited to watch the inevitable manhandling.

The nurses stood over her for a few seconds.

'Get her up. I'm not having this behaviour.'

They lifted her to her feet, gripping her under the arms and counting to three before they did so. They walked and she shuffled. Their bodies pressed close against her as they moved up the bright corridor, the momentum making her move forward whether she wanted to or not. How had this happened again? She wanted to scream and writhe in frustration but knew they would only grip her tighter – walk faster. Desperate, she started to cry. Since she had been on the medication, though, her eyes had been tearless. Constantly hot, itchy and blurred – like everything she looked at was a mirage on a desert horizon. So she dry-sobbed, screwing up her eyes and biting down a growing scream at the futility and loneliness of her plight. Sympathy had been in short supply recently. This kind of crying looked less than authentic to onlookers – provoking raised eyebrows and sighs of tired judgement.

Please make this all stop. Make it go away forever. She wanted help.

If she'd kept her eyes closed she wouldn't have seen him. Coming out of one of the rooms she was being ushered past was a doctor. No white coats here but they did wear ties. That's how you could tell a doctor. She had met him before and he had smiled and made faces like he was listening but made noises in all the wrong places like he was listening to someone else as well. He seemed kind enough.

She was not looking at the doctor though. She was looking at the man who walked with him. Out on the street you might walk past this man without thinking. Without seeing.

In here it was different. He stood out. He fitted right in and he didn't. He wasn't scared of the place and he wasn't above it either. Respectful but relaxed. She imagined that this man would carry himself just the same whether he were walking through Buckingham Palace or through his own living room.

He moved easily and freely. None of the psychic grime of the place seemed to stick to him.

She knew instantly that this man could help her. She knew this because he had helped her once before.

The man's name was Chris O'Brien.

1

It was the first day of spring, though you wouldn't know it. There'd been a hailstorm just that morning. It was over now but it had been spectacular whilst it lasted, rattling off the windowpanes, car bonnets and pavements – scattering pedestrians more effectively than a mounted police charge. The pigeon huddled outside on my window ledge still had its head pushed way down into its hunched wings from the onslaught and was looking well pissed off. More than just the normal bewildered disgruntlement you see on a pigeon's face. It looked ready to kick a sparrow. To death even.

Myself, I was pretty happy as far as it goes. It had been a good Christmas. I'd managed to burn off all the extra calories by shagging for England. Monogamously too.

Debra Prentice and I were an item. The thing that kept me at just pretty happy rather than elated was the fact that she had returned to university. I was visiting as regularly as work allowed, which had been pretty regular. The visits were expensive but worth it.

I had actually increased my fees. Everyone had told me that I should. I now cost £21.50 per hour. Perhaps 'Expensive but worth it' could be a slogan on my business cards. I had achieved some measure of notoriety of late. Picture in the papers and all. Paula Prescatta had phoned and advised me to get a stylist. Wasn't quite sure how to take that.

'Private Investigator Solves 13-year-old Murder.'

Who's too cool for school?

The big deal that the papers made out of that aspect had been incidental to me. I never shed a tear for the long dead parents of Gregory D'ancona. What I cared about was putting D'ancona away for seducing a fifteen-year-old girl so that he could destroy her father, for killing a young guy called Mark just because he was in the wrong place at the wrong time and for daring to lay a finger on my mate Kelp – who still suffered pains from the beating he took.

Still, I don't think I'd have got together with Debra – Kelp's sister – if it hadn't been for all the trial and tribulation. Every cloud...

To be honest, some of my regular law firm

19

work had been drying up despite the notoriety. They must have thought I was too 'big time' now. High profile. But, as I was about to discover, that's when you start to get the nutters.

Someone was knocking at my office door. I kept saying come in and they kept knocking until I had to shout 'ENTER!' so loudly the pigeon flew off.

The door cracked open and this little guy peeked his head round looking so wounded that I'd yelled at him. Not off to a good start.

'I'm sorry. I didn't mean to shout so loud. Please come in and sit down.'

Why was I apologising? I'm a sucker for wounded looks. Knight in Shining Armour Syndrome. If he'd been a woman I'd probably be pulling a chair out and mentally reducing my fee by now.

He did the 'I've never been in a PI's office before and I don't know where to put myself' shuffle. I've got three client chairs and they're arranged around the room in what I pretend to myself is a system of *Feng Shui* style psychological significance – whereby I can make initial judgements about prospective clients upon which chair they sit in and how long it takes them to decide.

He sat in the one furthest away from me.

The 'I'm intimidated by the whole experience' chair. It's also the least comfortable looking. The 'I'm not worthy' chair, if you will.

'How can I help you?' I enquired. Smiling a friendly smile.

Apart from the initial wounded look, he'd made very little eye contact with me so far, glancing round the room in a manner that could only be described as furtive.

I waited a while for him to answer. He just carried on with the furtive glancing, plus a little bit of throat clearing.

'How can I help you?' I repeated. A little slower, a little louder.

'I'm sorry I didn't make an appointment,' he said quietly.

'That's okay. You just happened to catch me between appointments.'

I didn't bother telling him how far in between.

'I saw the sign outside.'

'And here you are...'

I bet he hadn't seen the sign. A little brass plaque. Blink and you miss it. A slightly larger plaque above it announced the presence of the National Union of Pocket-Watch Menders. We both had offices located above a sandwich shop.

'I've seen you in the papers.'

See. Naff all to do with the sign.

'That's nice.'

'Can you help me?'

'*How* can I help you?'

Maybe if I just stuck with the same sentence and changed the emphasis on each word from time to time. No. If it carried on like this, I was just going to write it on a sheet of A4, fold it into an aeroplane, and throw it at him.

During the long wait before he spoke again I studied him. He was probably not a great deal older than me, maybe late thirties. He was not ageing well. Receding hairline, potbelly but stick thin limbs. There was an unhealthy malar flush on his upper cheeks. His eyes lacked any sparkle. He was relatively smartly dressed but had probably not changed in days. I could just smell him from where I was too. Stale sweat, and something else – which I could only describe as 'burnt'. If I'd been his employer and he'd turned up to work looking like this, I'd have sent him home. Finally he broke the silence.

'You might be the sort of man who can help...'

'If I live that long,' I muttered under my breath.

'I need someone who can help me.'

I picked up a pen and started writing. Before I got to the folding stage though, he spoke again:

'Can you follow someone?'

I put my pen down, screwed up the sheet of A4 and threw it deftly into the wastepaper basket. Direct hit. If only life were always like that. I sighed, somewhat dramatically, before speaking.

'Normally it's one of the things I do. But right now I'm having difficulty just following this conversation.'

'I'm sorry. This isn't easy for me. I've never done this before.'

'I understand, Mr...?'

'Oh, I'm sorry! Mr. Courtney. William Courtney. Call me Bill.'

'Bill. People have normally never been to see a private investigator before. I'm not going to shoot you or anything. Think of me as perhaps a solicitor, or something less intimidating. I can understand that this is not easy for you. I would imagine that's why you're here. You have a problem that you can't solve on your own. So let's make a start. Who would you like me to follow and why?'

'The police just turned me away. They

think I'm mad...'

'Bill. Who would you like me to follow and why?'

He gave a sort of half-smile. It looked rehearsed.

'The person I'd like you to follow ... is me.'

I purposefully ignored the element of drama he was trying to convey.

'Is it a bodyguard you're after? It's not really what I do. I know some people...'

He cut in on me, which was certainly a break from past performance.

'No no, you don't understand! It's not me who needs protecting.'

'Okay Bill. I'll remain silent. I'll listen to the rest of what you have to say. Then I'll tell you whether my help or advice will be appropriate to you or not.'

He took as deep a breath as his current state of health seemed to allow before continuing:

'People are in danger. People need protecting from *me*. I need someone who can stop me. It's the full moon you see...'

I thought I could see where this was going.

'Mr. Courtney. Can I stop you there please? You wouldn't, by any chance, be about to tell me that you are, in fact, a werewolf?'

Bill nodded eagerly, looked like he'd found

an understanding ear. I felt a little bit sorry for him, but I'd had it with psychiatry in my previous career and I didn't have time for this.

I sighed before continuing.

'I've decided my help will not be appropriate to you. Let me, however, offer you some advice...'

He looked at me, wide-eyed and expectant like a hungry puppy dog.

'Mind the door handle doesn't hit you in the arse on your way out.'

2

That's when the guy burst into tears.

Having said that, there were very few actual tears. His eyes were red and dry as if from previous blubbing episodes but his eyelids were now shuttering up and down uncontrollably as if trying to squeeze every last bit of moisture from his face and coming up short.

Then I saw what all that moisture was being used for. Mucous production. As his shoulders trembled he seemed to make an involuntary lumpy swallowing action and you could hear him gulp down a large lump of snot. The following sigh caused a great bubble of the stuff to issue from one nostril. Like you see on the children of the poor.

Bless him. I couldn't let him leave like this. I drew a tissue from the box on my windowsill and held it out in offering. He seemed like he didn't even notice me. I walked over to him and pressed it into his palm. Sweaty. His bodily fluids must have been having a tough time prioritising.

My act of kindness seemed to send his shoulders into further spasm, but the tears still would not come.

Time for a bit of honesty, by way of an apology. Self-disclosure is a legitimate counselling response. Offer the client something of yourself, generally an example of a situation you yourself have found difficult. Show them that vulnerability, fallibility, is okay:

'Bill, I've been a little sharp with you and I'm sorry. My fault. To be honest, I'm missing my girlfriend right now and it's got me preoccupied.'

The last part of my sentence was drowned out by a strangulated wail from Bill. It had started with a loud choke at the word 'missing' and continued well into the dead air that followed my pronouncement.

The wail ended with him throwing his head back and for a split second I actually thought he was going to howl. Instead he made a snot-laden sniff and swallow, then threw his head forward into his hands, where he cradled it for a while as he produced a series of rasping sobs until he was able to speak.

'My wife ... my wife left me,' he croaked.

'Oh.'

'Oh' is *not* a legitimate counselling response. It is too fallible. There is nothing wise or sage-like about it. It has no *gravitas*. Even a favourite swear word would be preferable.

'God, I miss her so much,' he gasped. He was shaking his head slightly now whilst still cradling it, with the effect that matted strands of his hair began to spike out from his head between his fingers.

Time to move on to reflective responding.

'With your wife gone, you feel desperate. Confused.' Better O'Brien. Better.

He nodded without looking up from his lap, his palms still wedded to his forehead and temples. The greasy hairdo was becoming distinctly New Wave by this point.

'I don't know what to do,' he said. Still no eye contact but at least his head stayed still. One hand came away from his hair and began to grip the arm of the chair in a telltale show of impotent frustration. A man desperate to regain control.

'I'm hearing that you feel the need to do *something*, Bill.'

God. I sounded like a parody of a counsellor. Maybe if I annoyed him enough he'd get up and slap me. Might be cathartic for him.

'I'll go mad if I don't do something.' He looked back up at me this time.

'What does that *mean* to you Bill? To be mad?'

How very Therapy. All I had to do now was grow a beard and sit on a beanbag.

'I can't cope. I can't handle it!'

He shook his head vigorously. His teeth gritted. His knuckles white from clinging to the chair. His cheeks redder from the rising heat of anxiety contrasting with the unhealthy pallor of the rest of his greyish green skin. The good thing was that he didn't seem about to blurt out any more stuff about full moons or silver bullets. The edge of drama and hint of manipulation seemed to have gone. Voicing the source of

28

his distress had grounded him back into reality for the time being.

I was around the front of my desk at this point, perching my backside against it after having offered the tissue. I sat down opposite him in the slightly more comfortable client chair, pulled it closer to him, and leaned in before speaking:

'Bill. You are coping. You might not be at your best right now – by a long stretch. But you are seeking help. You've come to the wrong place, and you're asking in the wrong way, but at least you are trying. It's a start. It's what you can build on.'

'The doctor couldn't do anything for me...'

'Probably gave you Amitriptyline? Dothiepin?'

'That's right,' he said, a little surprised. 'Dothiepin. It's not working...'

'It will take a few weeks before exerting an antidepressant effect. It's certainly not a cure for distress. Are you not sleeping, Bill?'

'Hardly. I just can't seem to switch off my mind...'

He seemed to have a way of making his sentences trail off into nowhere, his mouth still moving slightly after the words had gone.

'Constantly chewing things over,' I reflected.

He gave a little nod of assent. A forlorn nod.

'It must feel awful,' I empathised.

'Do you think I'm going mad?' he asked pleadingly.

'Bill. If things don't get any better for you then you could be running into bigger problems, but you don't strike me as suffering from psychosis.'

He nodded, letting me know that he understood the terminology, but I couldn't tell if he was pleased or disappointed by my diagnostic pronouncement.

'You're anxious, preoccupied and sleep deprived,' I continued. 'And that can all add up to some pretty strange thought processes. Hence, all that werewolf bollocks you were trying to persuade us both to believe.'

He looked like he wanted to protest for a moment, but I just kept talking.

'And you appear to have the underlying problem of chronic low self-esteem. Your choice of imagery suggests both anger and a psychological need to be seen as a powerful figure. Your wife leaving you must have been a very disempowering experience.'

He nodded and gulped before speaking.

'She was raped.'

This time I did swear, sort of under my breath.

Bill was just staring at the carpet now but he began to speak:

'It happened over a year ago now. I blamed myself that I wasn't able to protect her. I felt devastated. Numb.'

'As if you had been raped yourself...' I offered.

He looked at me. 'That's what she said. She got angry at me...'

'For not being able to support her?'

He nodded.

'And for behaving like you were the victim?'

He nodded again.

I felt sorry for the guy. I felt glad that his wife had left him too. Dealing with his emotional baggage because of the trauma she'd suffered would be no life for her.

'Can you help me?' The puppy dog eyes again.

'Yes.' I replied this time.

I explained that I would not be tracking down his missing wife for him. Nor would I be involving him in some detective type adventure that would help him get his groove back.

I told him to go see an acupuncturist or Chinese herbalist. Told him he was suffering from Kidney *Yin Xu* with Fire Blazing and God knows what else. Told him that practising a Martial Art would help to build his confidence and that if he was going to pursue some Chinese Medicine, then he might as well do a Chinese Martial Art as well. I didn't particularly want him at my *Wing Chun* class so I gave him the address of a *Lau Gar* fella who had started up some classes on the other side of town. I told him to eat chicken soup with fresh garlic and ginger.

Some might accuse me of being too directive. I like to think I'm practising a newer, snappier form of Solution Focused work. Call it *Rushed Therapy*. Might write a book entitled: *What's your Best Hope before I Kick you Out of Here?*

Anyway, it seemed to work because he had the appearance of someone truly motivated by the time I had finished with him.

As he left I shook his hand. It was less sweaty now. I noticed too that his knuckles were not the least bit hairy.

Just before he made the door I said, 'Bill.'

'Yes?'

'Bit of soap and water wouldn't go amiss either.'

Got a smile out of him.

3

The sun was out in earnest now. I could even feel it a little on the back of my neck as I stood in the middle of the room. I sauntered to the window and watched Bill Courtney car-dodge across the still damp street. He continued to cut a sad figure but I fancied there was something of a spring in his step now.

A job well done O'Brien. Would it spoil it to invoice him now?

The phone rang.

'O'Brien Investigations and Community Care Services,' I answered.

'OB. You got anything on?'

It was Debra. I love Debra. I particularly love the way she completely ignores me when I say stupid stuff. Behaviourist.

'My Calvin Kleins. And you...?'

'I do believe I have a pair of your Calvins on too.'

She was one of those women who steals your clothes.

'Be still my heart. Are you completing the *ensemble* with a sturdy sports bra?'

'No.'

'Are you wearing rope gold at a jaunty angle?'

'No.'

I could tell she wanted to laugh. For sure. She continued, 'If you are *less than busy* this weekend, why don't you ease on down the road and come see me?'

Odd. It was unlike her to request. I tended to suggest visits. Not that she ever turned me down though.

'And what would I want to trail all the way down to Londinium for?'

Like I needed an excuse.

'Thought we could compare underwear.'

'You'd win – hands down.'

'Hands down is what I had in mind.'

I got a warm tingle in what I'll politely describe as my *Tan Tien*.

'You've persuaded me. That can't be why you've called, Debs. What's up?'

'By now, both your dick and your curiosity!'

'By God lady, you're in a playful mood, aren't you?'

'No. Just don't want to waste my credit explaining. Talk when you get here. You are the sweetest link – goodbye.'

Well, well, well.

It was Friday lunchtime. All I had to do was go home and see to the cat. In the highly unlikely event that Mrs. Danvers – my redoubtable cat looker-after – was away, then I'd just leave a note, a whole tin in the bowl and a shit-load of dry food too. It's been done before.

No way did I want to hit the rush when I got down there so I'd kill some time before setting off. I knew what I'd do. That little episode with Bill had inspired me to visit a friend who I'd been neglecting to pop in on lately. His name was Asif Hasan, an SHO – that's a doctor – based at Lindlea Heights, the local psychiatric facility.

I went downstairs to the sandwich shop. They know me well now so they're willing to be a bit more creative with their ingredients in my honour. I had white crab meat and iceberg lettuce with a lemon and olive oil vinaigrette and a ham and Gruyere with honeyed mustard. Both in bagels. They weren't into the whole *halal* thing so I got Asif an egg mayonnaise. I asked for alfalfa in it but they said I was pushing it.

Then I took the back way round, driving up Emm Lane in Heaton – the leafy suburb of Bradford. Impressive houses. Where the mill owners and merchants would have lived in Edwardian opulence. The capillary streets were still residential – probably accountants – but along the main artery were nursing homes and hollowed out student flats. There was even a bail hostel that I knew of, but they kept themselves to themselves.

Parking thankfully wasn't a problem. Psychiatry is popular with the impoverished so most hospital visitors took the bus. Before long I was standing in the recently souped-up reception area, explaining to a security guard why he should let me in.

'You haven't got an outpatient's appointment,' he informed me. The tail and the wing tip of what was undoubtedly a swallow in flight were just peeking over the top of his crisp white shirt collar.

'No,' I said. Holding up my sandwich bag. 'But please bleep Dr. Hasan and tell him I have a delivery of *corpus luteum/albumen* compound for urgent oral administration.'

He eyed me suspiciously.

'You work the door at Zeds, don't you?'

I shrugged and spread my hands nonchalantly. I'd intended to look cool but I nearly dropped the sandwich.

'I tried to get work there,' he paused. 'Nowt happening.'

We were pretty exacting about whom we took on.

'Well, you've been most courteous with me. I'll put in a word for you,' I beamed.

He buzzed me through.

Asif was just finishing his last appointment. He smiled and shook my hand immediately in the Asian manner before turning and striding off up the corridor whilst I listened to both the rustling of his trouser material and watched the back of his head.

'Follow me up to Badlands. Many discharge summaries to do, but it will be quieter up there.'

Originally the wards had all been numbered but, along with the refurb, some tosspot had given them names like *Birchgrove* and *Ashlands*. That'd help. Might as well give the psychiatrists names like *Jack in the Green* and *Herne the Hunter* while you're at it.

'Bought you lunch, but it looks like you could do without it.'

Asif gestured dismissively as he walked ahead of me. 'I lead a sedentary lifestyle. Thus I am doomed.'

I liked the way he said it so cheerily. I liked the way he clearly pronounced all four syllables in the word 'sedentary'.

As we walked onto the ward known by the staff as *Badlands*, the nursing assistant at the tiny reception desk gave me a look like 'What's *he* doing here?' But I was obviously accompanying a doctor so he wasn't about to challenge me.

We entered a little side room further up the corridor and I chucked the paper sandwich bag on top of a thick pile of medical notes on the desk whilst Asif pulled his chair up to face them. He deftly ripped open the bag and tore the sandwich into quarters.

'So, how is the world of private investigation?' he said before taking a measured bite.

'Oh, you know. Kicking butts, taking names.'

'Who would have thought you'd started out in a caring profession?'

'I prefer this. I get to help genuinely unhappy people – *practical* help – and if I don't like the bullshit story I'm being sold then I show them the door.'

'Yes,' he said dreamily, 'I would like to have been a surgeon.'

He was joking, of course. The Mind was his fascination.

We spent much of the afternoon talking psychiatric bollocks. I don't find medics particularly interesting but Asif has a penchant for the obscure so we'd been naturally drawn to each other during the time we'd crossed professional paths. He'd told me I was the only nurse he'd ever met who'd heard of Wilhelm Reich. I'd told him he was the only psychiatrist I'd met who had too.

If you want to know anything about *Lesch-Nyhan's* or *Ganser's Syndrome* – ask Asif. He was wasted in the NHS. He should have his own TV show.

Well, I'd watch it.

'What's your take on *Lycanthropy?*'

'Lycanthropy? It should be no surprise to you that I have never come across such a case. It is not a diagnosis in itself.' He paused and wiped a crumb from his lip before continuing, 'Rather, it is a mono-symptomatic delusion within a person who has other features of psychosis, usually with a depressive element. I would be loathe to include it in any diagnostic pronouncement if I ever see a case.'

'Why's that, Asif?'

'The belief that one is or is capable of becoming a wolf? I do not consider it a delusion.'

'You mean you believe it can happen?'

'Not at all! And I think you know what I mean, Chris. I think werewolves are so much a part of popular culture that, although such a belief can properly be said to be *falsely held*, it could no longer be considered to be *out of keeping with one's cultural or educational background*. Psychiatry would not touch it. The same can be said for vampires or New Age gurus. They have their own organisations and websites. Let them believe what they like.'

'What if they start acting out the belief?'

'Running round biting people? Then the Mental Health Act might be invoked – but I would favour the Criminal Justice System.'

'That, or the dog warden.'

I described to Asif my meeting with Bill Courtney that morning. He listened with interest but also took the opportunity to finish his egg sandwich.

'Mmmm,' he said after I had finished speaking. 'Of course here it is not just mono-symptomatic. With the mood disturbance we could maybe go for *Schizo-Affective Disorder*. I agree with you that there is grandiosity in

40

the way he expressed his belief. But it sounded like you almost talked him out of it – an overvalued idea rather than a delusion. Would you like to refer this gentleman?'

I snorted then spoke.

'No Asif. Let's just let this one *slip through the net*, as they say.'

Our small talk became ever smaller as the conversation drew to a natural and comfortable close.

I felt relaxed and happy. At ease with the world and gestating a small sparkling pearl of anticipatory bliss somewhere in my belly, like an inward smile. The kind of feeling you get when the week is over, you've got all your work finished and you plan to hit the pubs in the next couple of hours – your mates will be there, you've got money in your pocket and a whole load of gossip or funny stories to hand around. That sort of thing.

I was going to see Debra.

So that's the way I was feeling when Asif offered to walk down to reception with me, to protect me from the dirty looks reserved for former employees. Not that I was bothered, but I gracefully accepted his company.

As we exited the office door and started

up the corridor there was a commotion going on in front of us. A young lady was being *moved & handled* down the corridor towards us. The staff must have been on a recent refresher course because they were very good at it – all moving in the same direction and everything.

We just stood back as they passed. It wasn't the kind of situation a medic and a visitor were going to get involved in.

The woman didn't appear to be struggling – just too weak and tired to walk, too upset to think straight. Poor lass. I shot her a sympathetic look. Our eyes met.

And I recognised her.

Before I could react in any way other than my jaw dropping to the floor, her entourage whisked her out of sight around the right hand corner of the 'T' shaped ward.

I could tell she had recognised me too. Her eyes had screamed my name though her mouth was unable. The sparkling pearl in my belly had suddenly become the size and weight of a clenched fist.

But what could I do? Race after them and rescue her? Start throwing nurses out of the windows?

For the brief time that I had worked in that hospital myself, the feeling of *powerlessness* had hung over me like a spectre. Wanting desperately to help people but, more often than not, being prevented from doing so by the fear of overstepping professional boundaries. Having to play by other people's rules. Working in the community had given me more scope, more autonomy, but only a little.

I had laid that demon to rest with my new career. Or so I'd thought. One visit to the Heights was all it took to make me feel angry and small once more.

'Was that Linzi Delaney?' I asked Asif, as I forced my feet to work again and we headed for the ward exit.

'Linzi Morgan. Her married name was Delaney. You know her?'

'I worked with her before.'

We walked down the main corridor in silence. I could have asked Asif what the situation was. Professional though he was, he would have told me. He would have told me how she came to be admitted, what treatment she was receiving, how her behaviour was on the ward. But I didn't want to know right now. There was a danger I might not be able to tear myself away.

At reception Asif shook my hand again and said, 'Now is not the time, Chris. Your friend was obviously sedated. But I am sure you will want to visit her when you return from London. Put it from your mind. We will look after her.'

It was what I wanted to hear. I wanted the pearl back. I wanted to enjoy driving down the M1 in the setting sun, scanning the rolling landscape for the blossoms of spring. I wanted to go shag my girlfriend.

So I put Linzi Delaney from my mind.

I don't know that I'll ever forgive myself for that.

4

Driving my recently acquired motor was still a guilty pleasure. The car had been a gift from Mr. Trevini, who remained extremely grateful to me for rescuing his daughter. My beloved black Escort had been trashed by a couple of heavies down in Dorset but Trevini had replaced it with a new one. Numerous trips down south had added over 5K to the mileage since Christmas but it was still an absolute joy to look at the clock and think of all the years and miles to go

44

before bits started dropping off.

It was like having a teenage girlfriend.

But hey, having a twenty-six-year-old girlfriend was good enough for me. The miles between us weren't ideal but I wasn't complaining. The journey to see her had become an enjoyable ritual of anticipation. Driving at a conservative 80, except for where I knew there to be speed cameras, I would listen to Tamla-Motown, sing loudly in that uninhibited way that lone driving and lack of traffic lights allows, and my thoughts would be of Debra only.

Normally.

Tonight I was a little more sombre. I had a CD of Tori Amos playing hauntingly melodic piano cover versions – 'Angie' by the Stones and 'Teen Spirit' by Nirvana. I kept repeating the same tracks.

I was thinking about Linzi Delaney.

I had first met her when I was a community psychiatric nurse. She'd been sent to us by her G.P. because she had burst into tears in his surgery. It was what we used to call an 'inappropriate referral' – such a display of emotion should not automatically be taken as evidence of a mental health problem requiring specialist input. But when you met Linzi you could see why the doctor had wanted to do anything in his power to help.

She was beautiful.

She would have bought out the rescuer in the most world-weary of cynics. She would inspire the tone deaf to sing. And yes, she would give a saint a hard on. There was something about her that would have made *anyone* do *anything* for her.

Except, for some reason, her twat of a husband.

I guess the reason was that he was a Delaney. There is no Irish Mafia in Bradford as such but, if there were, 'Stick' Delaney would be the Godfather. In Leeds it would have been Denny Maguire. There was some cross-pollination, and some other respected clans, but being an O'Brien didn't amount to a whole hill of spuds up here. I'd always be London Irish.

Anyway. Stick had a grandson called Rob. Rob had a wife called Linzi. To say he did not treat her right is an understatement. I'll tell you a little about it although I'm shaking with pure anger as I recall the tale she told me.

She told me falteringly and through tears, but with a compassion for her husband that I did not feel he deserved.

Rob was full of confidence. Full of himself, some might say. Right from being a young lad he was strong and handsome and powerful. Being a Delaney was power enough in itself but that kind of reputation doesn't normally have the same ramifications until you hit pub-going age. For Rob that was about fourteen years old, but up until then he was king of the playground on his own merit anyway.

They had met at school. She was Miss Popular and he was Mister Hard. Cock of his year. It was inevitable that they would get together. Irrelevant whether Rob had actually fancied her – the fact that all the other boys wanted her meant that he had to have her.

Marriage and pregnancy followed. Kids never did. Being thrown down the stairs and hoofed in the stomach on a regular basis tends to interfere with your chances of going to full term.

It transpired that Linzi had miscarried for the third time just before I met her. She had been bleeding for a few days – hence the visit to the G.P.

She had been too scared to confide in anyone about her home situation. When her tears forced themselves to the surface in that doctor's surgery she became even more scared. Frightened that she couldn't control herself. Frightened that if she couldn't stop the tears then she might not be able to stop the words from blurting out either. Frightened because Rob had made it clear he would kill her if she did talk to anyone.

She agreed a nurse could come and see her at home because that seemed like the easiest way to just get out of that surgery and away from that doctor's concerned gaze. That's where I came in.

She spent all her time before my visit trying to think of stories to fob me off with and also stuff to tell the neighbours if anyone saw me. Rob was away on one of his frequent 'trips' but she was wary of any comeback if he ended up hearing that she'd had a visitor.

None of it worked. Before my coffee was half gone she was beginning to open up to me.

I was a good nurse. People talked to me. Often, the things they told me were very distressing – to them and to me. It was only when I couldn't stop myself acting on some of the distressing information that I fell foul of the profession. Sometimes I did more than just listen. Sometimes I stepped in and changed things. Things that they wanted to change but hadn't a hope in hell of doing by themselves. You can Enable, Facilitate and Advocate all you bloody well like. But sometimes people want you to *Champion* their cause for them. So that's what I did. Apparently though, that made me a bad nurse.

Still got my registration though. Not that I use it. I'd rather work the door of a nightclub than do agency shifts in a nursing home now but I keep it to prove a point. They couldn't take it away from me.

Anyway, I digress.

I sat with Linzi and listened to tales of drunkenness and cruelty. I think I pulled off 'concerned yet non-judgemental' – all the time wishing that this bastard Rob would walk through the door shouting the odds and give me an excuse to tear him a new arsehole.

When I left, it was clear that she had benefited from talking and wished to do it again. In the hallway, her body did that awkward thing of tying itself up in knots. I could tell she was about to hug me, but couldn't physically do it. Then it looked like she was going to shake my hand, but that didn't happen either. Finally, she grabbed at an open packet of Maltesers from off the telephone table and pushed a single one of the chocolates into my hand.

'Thanks, Linzi. I shall treasure this,' I had replied. It was something we had a laugh about on occasion.

That was the only time we met at the house. We had a number of other sessions together. We went to places that made it unlikely we would be spotted by anyone in her social circle. *Nice* places. We'd go for walks in the woods where she could cry if she wanted to. Shout and shake and throw stones if she wanted to. When she'd got more of a lid on things, we'd go to quiet restaurants together. We'd drink wine. Is that unprofessional too?

It helped Linzi to share what went on behind closed doors. It helped her to share how she felt about it. Eventually, it helped her to share the reason *why*.

You see, Rob had a dark secret. Something he was struggling with that made him such a tortured, violent soul. *Ahhh!* Get your fucking violins out.

Rob Delaney liked to have sex with men.

He wasn't gay. Rob hated 'queers'. Hated everything about them. There was no place within the Delaney family for such an abomination. Even if the Delaneys had been a warm and fluffy and tolerant family, he'd have felt the same though. Openly gay men made him cringe. Made him clench his fists until his fingers were bloodless and sensation departed. He hated women too. He hated flowers. He hated femininity.

He'd never take it either, only give it out. He hated the thought of anyone doing it to him. Didn't want some lithe young lad either. He wanted to be on top of a big, hairy man's man.

It sounded to me like he had a problem with *beauty*. A shame really, because he was good looking. He'd have made a successful gay man. Maybe that was the source of his frustration – his social standing just wouldn't have allowed it.

In order not to let his secret out, he had to travel far and wide to indulge in anonymous sex. That's what his 'trips' were. Let everyone think he was just being unfaithful. The Delaney's never really had a problem with that kind of behaviour. That was normal. It wasn't as if anyone would dare tell his wife anyway.

But his wife was the only one who knew the truth. She knew because he told her everything. In great detail too, frothing at the mouth as he did so, incensed and lustful, spitting words of horror into her face. Shouting at her to look him in the eye while he was talking to her, screeching at her when she did look. He'd pace around the room as she stood frozen to the spot whilst he talked about his conquests. He'd rush at her without warning and press his face into hers as he spoke. He'd order her to sit down then yell at her to stand up – or just drag her to her feet. Sometimes he'd break down at these times and sob with frustration. She had learnt early on not to go to him and offer him comfort. To touch him while he was crying would trigger an explosion of the most sickening violence.

When he had finished, he would always wait for her to sleep. Then he would wake her and whisper to her in a tone which could sound almost tender. He would always say, 'I'll kill you if you talk.' Sometimes on these occasions he would still have sex with her. Sometimes it would even be vaginal, but only ever from behind.

She said it had not always been like that. He had grown dark and distant gradually. She could always tell he wasn't that interested in sex but he could perform well enough. She put everything down to the drink at first. The Delaney's were a drinking family. She used to pray for a child – hoping that would ease the growing distance between them, straighten Rob out and give him meaning. She knew that the family were always eagerly awaiting great-grandchildren. She could see that Rob was pressured by this though he wouldn't admit it.

They had been together four years. The violence didn't start until the second year. Rob's disclosures about his sexual activities had only started to come out in the last twelve months.

Linzi felt trapped. She accepted now that nothing was going to magically change her situation for the better. She realised that she could never be happy if she stayed in this relationship. She could see that she might well end up dead in this relationship. But the prospect of death seemed far more real and imminent were she to make any attempt to leave.

In between my talks with Linzi, I made it my business to know all I could about Rob Delaney. I watched him. I followed him. I knew where he drank. What he drank. How much he could hold before he had to take a piss, and what hand he held his dick in when he did. In short, I became a detective.

I didn't know why I was doing it. At first I just wanted to see what this monster looked like. I fantasised about following him into the bogs or down an alley, walling him up and telling him his days of wife beating were over.

Couldn't do that. Even if I won the initial confrontation, he wasn't going to leave it there. I'd have to kill him. Then I'd have to kill all the Delaney's. Then all the Maguire's for good measure in case I'd offended anyone. Quite possibly somewhere along the line the Irish Republican Army would get involved and it would all just get a bit silly.

Perhaps someone else could talk to Rob for me. Someone to whom he would listen. So with trembling legs and an arsehole that felt like Rob had been at it, I walked into the lair of Stick Delaney.

The guy must have been pushing eighty but still looked as scary as two gorillas injecting each other with steroids. His pool hall cronies weren't exactly matinee idols either. But I held onto my stomach and bowel contents, took a deep breath of the stale smoky air, and set my stall out.

I told him it was concerning his grandson. I told him which one. I asked him if he wanted anyone else present whilst I said what I had to say.

We ended up in a smaller room, sat round a poker table. Me, Stick and two heavy guys in their forties or fifties. They turned out to be Rob's father and uncle.

I told them I was a nurse. I didn't bother to mention what type of nurse I was. I said that Linzi had been rushed into hospital after collapsing in the street. I laid it on thick about 'trying to save the baby'. That the doctors could tell she had injuries from sustained and regular beatings. The hospital staff could tell it was domestic violence but Linzi wouldn't talk. Appalled as they were by her injuries, the hospital had hired a private detective to gather evidence on Rob so that they would have a strong case to take to the police and prosecute him.

I played up my Irish Catholic upbringing, told them I thought it was wrong to hit a woman – to which they all nodded sagely – but that I knew the Delaneys to be a 'good family' who should be able to sort out their own affairs without the feckin' law getting involved. They nodded again.

I said they should also tell Rob that this detective had followed him to various parts of the country. The inside word was that he hadn't found out what young Rob was up to yet, but soon might. I said I didn't much care if it was drugs or guns or what but that Rob should be careful.

Then I told them that I knew for a fact that, in such cases, the hospital would drop the matter and stop paying the detective if it came to their attention that divorce proceedings were under way. They had no wish to waste public money if they knew she was doing something about it herself.

They thanked me, and then asked me to leave.

No one shoved a screwdriver in my back on the way out. That, by the way, was how he'd got the name 'Stick' – it was what he favoured for sticking in people.

A couple of days later, I was in a bar in Girlington. A man approached me and asked me to sit with him. Polite but uncompromising. When we were sitting comfortably, the landlord bought over two creamy pints of Guinness. No money changed hands.

He told me that the family was grateful for the tip off. Linzi was 'a lovely girl' and didn't deserve all this. They all respected her for not being a grass into the bargain. Rob had been given quite a beating by his dad and his uncle. He would go nowhere near Linzi ever again or he would risk much more of the same. Rob had been only too keen to arrange a divorce under the circumstances. The guy downed his Guinness, slapped my back, and departed.

God, did I feel pleased with myself. They swallowed every word of it. Have you heard the one about the thick Irishman?

Sure, I could do this kind of thing for a living.

I saw Linzi a couple of times after that. She said she hadn't realised that people like me existed. Said she couldn't think of any way to repay me.

Seeing as I fancied the arse off her I could certainly think of one thing. But it would have been wrong for me to exploit her gratitude to get my end away. I'm not *that* unprofessional.

So I pondered a little longer on what might have been. I agonised unproductively about what fate had befallen Linzi to bring her into contact with psychiatric services again. I listened to some more morbid piano sounds.

By Watford Gap though, I had pretty much had enough of being sombre and my thoughts turned back to Debra and Freakpower's *Drive Thru Booty* graced my sound system. By the time I peeled off onto the north circular, I was fair squirming in my seat.

Debra lived in a shared house in Hornsey. She shared with three other students, none of whom were too annoying. Apart from being a student of Japanese language and literature herself, Debra was working part time as a security guard at an art gallery. She also taught a women's self defence class, but I don't think she charged for that.

I managed to find a parking space without too much hassle. Same street and everything.

She answered the door wearing only a very short dark green towel. Her light coffee skin was dry but her hair was still slightly damp. Her smell was white musk. Always. I kept some at home myself to fill up my senses from time to time but it wasn't the same. Her body seemed to add a magical bass tone to the scent itself.

She smiled. Beamed, rather. 1000 watts.

'Nice towel,' I ventured.

We kissed on the doorstep before I entered the hall. Debra turned and led the way through to the kitchen. I watched her move. Being a detective, I detected the fine rolling motion of her backside beneath the towel. Like two bowling balls being carried in a pillowcase. I ached for her.

'I've aired you some wine,' she said as she poured from the open but full bottle and handed me the glass. She wasn't one of those women for whom uncorking was a mystery – even though she didn't drink. She never had to hand me a jar of olives to get the lid off for her either.

I sipped the fruity Temperanillo. Decent.

'Just you in?' I asked. The house seemed quiet.

'Uh huh,' she responded with a slow nod of her precious head.

I put down my wine. I swept the work surface with the palm of my hand to clear away any stray crumbs.

Then I lifted her up, sat that girl in front of me, and ate her.

5

After I'd had my starter, so to speak, we dined out at an all night noodle bar in Islington that was straight out of *Tampopo*. Ramshackle trendy. I had various parts of various seagoing creatures dipped in *wasabi* paste and *soy*. Each mouthful with thinly sliced pickled ginger. Debra had every type of vegetable *tempura* going, a *miso* soup and *tofu* marinated in something hot and salty.

I had a *Sapporo* beer. Debra had gunpowder tea.

I asked her what she'd invited me down for but she just said, 'Tomorrow morning.'

We strolled into an amusement arcade after the meal and kicked each other's asses on *Tekken 3* and *Dead or Alive*. Then we went across to Stoke Newington and a secluded dance hall that was pumping out live music. Real music. I was one of only a few white faces in the joint but it didn't seem like a big deal.

It was great. The drums rattled like they were going to fall apart and roll into the crowd. The Hammond organ flickered between a purr and a growl, and the alto sax blew like an aviation fuel explosion. The singer gave a cracking version of Jnr Walker's 'How Sweet it is to be Loved by You' whilst we danced and mouthed the words to each other. The floor even seemed to clear a little around us. The absolute high point came as we were just about to leave the floor. The singer whipped a harmonica from his pocket, the bass cakewalked, the guitar jangled, as they launched into Stevie

Wonder's 'I was Made to Love Her'. The tambourine just tickled around the edges of it all and we danced on.

Like a sweet magnolia tree – my love blossoms, tenderly.

Transcendent.

Later, smoothing across a cool bed sheet, under a quilt that felt like a mother's arms, we made love slowly whilst the urban songbirds offered up a dawn chorus that spoke of the impossibility of defeat.

She gave me until the dot of 10 am, which surprised me.

'Hope you brought your kit,' she said as I opened my eyes.

'I can't believe I just shagged my P.E. teacher! How much did I drink?'

'No more than usual. Hands off cocks and on socks, OB. We're running.'

'Have you ever considered a career in the army?' I joked.

'That bunch of pussies?' she sneered.

God, I loved her.

Finsbury park is huge. I guess that everything is relative but avoid having to run round it unless you've got heavy sponsorship.

Actually, I loosened up after about a mile and a half and it wasn't so bad. That's when another runner pulled along beside us.

He was about a thousand times blacker than Debs. Half a foot taller than me. He had the shoulders of a boxer and the legs of a marathon runner.

And he was barefoot.

'Geoffrey...' nodded Debra.

'Debra...' he nodded back.

He glanced at me and said, 'Pleased to meet you O'Brien. We will talk.'

I just nodded and we all carried on running. We silently tested each other out like athletes do. I was no athlete but I tried my best.

I came third.

We finished up doing some warm-down stretches in a children's play area. I thought he might well have been a boxer. There were some healing scars on his face as if from recent battle. As he leant forward at one point though, his T-shirt reared up to reveal an equally recent scar on his lower back. It ran vertical rather than horizontal like a rope burn would. Not a boxing injury then. His feet, however, were pristine.

'I'm impressed,' I said. Looking down at Geoffrey's feet.

'You should try it. Better than any running shoe.'

'I can't see it happening. In my line of work I often pretend to be tying my laces.'

He stuck out his large bony hand for me to shake. So we did.

'My name is Geoffrey Sitcha. Thank you for seeing me Mr. O'Brien,' he said.

'Hell, wasn't much I could do about it was there?' I could sense Debra's eye twinkling. 'And drop the *mister*,' I added. 'You had me looking behind to see if you were talking to my dad.'

We rubbed down with a towel from Debra's backpack and I added a denim shirt to my T-shirt and track trousers. Geoffrey donned a pair of trainers taken from his backpack. I ask you?

We walked on to a café on Seven Sisters Road. I think it was Moroccan. The coffee had a distinctive muddy texture but tasted weaker than it looked.

It was time to find out what was going on.

'Geoffrey. Would it be fair to assume that this meeting is about some investigative work you would like me to do?'

'That is correct. Didn't Debra tell you anything?'

We both looked over at her. She was back at the counter getting herself a second coffee already. As she approached the table again she seemed to know she had become the subject of conversation.

'The reason that I didn't tell you anything, OB, was that I wanted you to hear it all straight from Geoffrey. See what you think. See how you feel. I was angry about what happened to Geoffrey and I wanted to help him. I think you can help him better than anyone else can. You might disagree. You might not want to take the case. I didn't want you saying yes just to make me happy.'

'Okay Debs. I'll buy that. But you must have thought that what Geoffrey's gonna tell me would make me agree anyway.'

'I'd like to think so,' she said.

'So, Geoffrey. What happened to you?'

'Some people tried to kill me.'

I steadied my initial shock behind a sip of coffee and tried to act as if I dealt with stuff like this all the time. 'I'm very sorry to hear that. Do you know these people? Do you know what their motive might have been?'

'It was a racially motivated attack. I had not met these people before. I would like you to find them if you can.'

'Isn't there a police investigation?'

Geoffrey Sitcha snorted. 'They can do nothing!'

'Geoffrey. That's not what I asked. Is there

64

an investigation or not?'

'I went to the police. I gave them all the details I could. Nothing has happened.'

I drew breath.

'Okay. You give me all the details you can and we'll see what we have to work with.'

Debra pulled a notepad and a pen from her rucksack and handed them to me with a smile. I mouthed 'Be Prepared' at her. She shrugged and said,

'Remember the seven P's.'

I did. Prior Preparation and Planning Prevents Piss Poor Performance. I hoped she was going to become my business partner when she finished Uni. Together, we could be big in Japan.

I listened and took notes whilst Geoffrey Sitcha spoke. He was a student at the School of Oriental and African Studies – that's where he knew Debra from. He was from Zimbabwe. He had no time for what Robert Mugabe was doing to his country so he was very pleased to be in the U.K. He felt it was important, however, for the Zimbabwean community over here to keep strong and supportive links with each other. He was especially interested in aiding refugees who may not have the same command of English language, customs and laws as he himself enjoyed. He had learnt, some eight weeks ago, that a large group of Zimbabwean asylum seekers, some of them as much victims of the 'land reforms' as their white business partners, had moved into a block of flats on an estate in south London.

He had been told that this group of people were scared to leave the building for fear of racist abuse and assault. All their London relatives were also scared to visit them there. Consequently, they found themselves very isolated.

Geoffrey had decided to visit these people. Tell them to hold their heads up high and not live in fear. Get them linked into the health care and benefits system. Help them get established.

But as he strode proudly and purposefully up one of those piss-stinking stairwells in that cold concrete maze, he was prevented from carrying out his good deed.

A gang of white males descended upon him. Well, literally speaking they also *ascended*. They came from in front and behind on the stairs. Too numerous to count or indeed to fight off. They overwhelmed him – and not just with their abusive language.

They dragged Geoffrey down the stairs.

This took some time due to the sheer amount of bodies cramped into the confined space, the number of times they paused to kick and stomp at his body along the way, and the fact that he had already climbed nine flights before they attacked him.

When there were no more stairs to descend and he lay in a growing pool of his own warm blood on the cold stone of the ground floor hallway, they kicked him some more. Harder this time – having more space to swing their vicious legs.

Geoffrey was obviously a strong lad with a fighting spirit. He knew how to duck and cover and he had remained conscious this whole time. He remembered them stripping him of his clothes, urinating on him. Then, in a mockery of assistance, they *cleaned* him. With bleach. As it burned into the lacerations on his naked body he tried to imagine he was blazing with the fire of vengeance, that he would be able to rise up and kill them all. But then he did finally pass out – consciousness choking away from him in urgent bursts as they turned him over and forced him to drink the bleach.

It is saddening – but perhaps not surprising at all – that, despite the duration of this ordeal, the amount of noise generated, and the fact that it happened in an ostensibly *public* place, no one came to his assistance.

No more than a few minutes could have passed before Geoffrey's eyes blinked slowly open and his brain started to process information again. He was beyond pain now – there had been so much of it that it would no longer register. Not much else had time to register before he felt himself rolling and falling, bouncing – then rolling again. Then he was up on two feet and running.

It ought not to have been possible. But survival has a way of forcing the issue.

Pain started to return. At least to his throat and lungs. The rest of his body worked beyond itself. Adrenalin kept his heart beating and his muscles contracting with the force of life. His senses seemed superhuman at this time. They told him everything he needed to stay alive.

Soon he was hiding in long, dark marsh grass – fed by the nearby Thames. He could hear his pursuers around him, thrashing wildly. He knew he could not be found. If he stayed still they could come within inches and would walk straight past, so frantic they were. If he had his strength he could silently ambush each one of them in turn. He came from Zulu warrior people. He understood grass. He grew up amongst the grasses. Safe here. It was concrete and staircases that were alien to him.

They were far in the distance now.

He passed out again. A pair of fluorescent-jacketed council workers, conducting an ecological survey, found him early the next morning. Barely alive. No less than a miracle.

Geoffrey Sitcha told me he had been out of hospital nearly four weeks now.

Reflecting on his escape, he believed that it had been his attacker's intention to drag him along behind a van in the same manner that racists in Texas had used to kill a fellow human being. He believed that he had been pushed from the back of a vehicle before it had a chance to build up much speed, and that his bonds had come loose.

When I'd finished listening my throat was dry and my palms damp. My voice cracked when I told Geoffrey how glad I was that he was alive to tell his story. I shook his hand again. Very tightly.

Then I told him that I would find these people.

I'm always making these rash promises. I should have a word with myself.

I felt Debra's hand resting upon my

forearm now. The touch was saying a multitude of things. I turned to her.

'So, Debs. What makes you think I'm the best man for the job?'

'You're white.'

'So what? Am I the only white guy you know?'

'You're the only white private investigator I know.'

'I'm still a sex machine to all the chicks.'

She ignored me and added, 'And you've got that Aryan thing going on...'

I suppose I did have that blond-haired, blue-eyed Nordic look. Vikings must have invaded Ireland once upon a time.

'So you think I've got what it takes to go under cover with the neo-nazis?'

'Maybe, you shaved your head...'

'As if!' I said.

6

When we left the café, Geoffrey Sitcha said, 'That coffee was shit. Where is there a Starbucks?'

We went back up to Islington.

I was calorie hungry by then so I had a blueberry bagel with cream cheese. Debra had a flapjack after determining that it was vegan, and Geoffrey had three slices of date and walnut cake. We all had espressos, but mine was a chaser to a frappucino. It all cost an absolute bomb, but I think that's part of the attraction.

'Is Geoffrey a Zulu name then?' I enquired cheekily.

'No, but that is the name I have used throughout my schooling and it's on my passport.'

Debra chipped in, 'When you told him you were Zulu, I could see OB thinking of Michael Caine and Pith helmets.'

'I'll have my man clean your kit!' enunciated Geoffrey in the clipped tones of a British officer.

'You like that movie?'

'Very much – if you can see past the inherent racism.'

'That's exactly how I feel about the sexism in *Get Carter* and *The Italian Job*.'

'It doesn't make them bad movies,' agreed Geoffrey.

Debra excused herself, thoughtfully placing another two coffees in front of us before she went. She obviously had no interest in the

71

way the conversation was developing.

The location developed into a pub and the coffee developed into lager. A clock on the wall was saying 2pm and I was saying,

'No, no. *Blame It On Rio* was his worst movie – but he performed as best he could, given the character and plot. He was just miscast. *On Deadly Ground* was his worst performance.

'No, no, no,' countered Geoffrey. 'How can you say that? His performance there was not essentially different than in *Mona Lisa*, he was just entirely let down by the supporting cast and the script.'

I still had the notepad that Debra had given me. I wrote BOLLOCKS! in large letters across one blank page and then held it up in front of Geoffrey's face whilst I drained my pint.

He laughed and finished his pint too. Then he made his apologies and left, saying he had a lot of academic work to catch up on. I bet he had. We hadn't discussed my fee, but somehow I got the idea that he wasn't an impoverished student.

I got myself a re-fill and sat looking at the scrabblings I'd made earlier. Details had been difficult to gather and it was hard to know exactly what my focus was going to be. It wasn't like looking for a missing person.

But I had clarified a few things with Geoffrey – in amongst the banter. He was interested in me gathering 'intelligence' on the racist thugs operating in the area where he had been assaulted. He thought we might be able to present this information to the police. I told him it was likely that they already had 'intelligence' – it was *evidence* that would be the problem. Geoffrey had just shrugged at that.

I told him what I thought. I thought that he was probably hoping to do something himself with any information I could give him. Either to empower the local community in defending itself against the threat or in order to exact his own personal revenge. He had shrugged again.

I chewed the top of the pen. Hope Debra didn't want it back. I flipped onto a fresh page of the pad and wrote INTELLI-GENCE, then underlined it three times. Then I drew Fat Freddy's Cat but didn't make his tail bushy enough. In trying to correct it I then made it too bushy.

I got another pint. Kronenbourg 1664 – the daddy of daytime drinking lagers. I sat back down and wrote on my pad:

Here comes O'Brien, like a bat out of hell
Someone gets in his way, someone don't feel so
well.

It made me feel better, anyway. Confidence building.

The barmaid was taking an interest. She leaned over from behind her breasts – sorry, the bar – and asked me what I was writing.

'Poetry,' I replied.

I decided that a visit to the police might help. Couldn't hurt. Well, it could if I presented myself in this state. I was a little too relaxed. I'd save it for Monday.

What I did do though was get a train from Highbury and Islington down to North Woolwich, and then took a ferry ride across the Thames. The grey water churned and foamed as we cut across its natural flow, flecks of it spraying up at me as I leant over the rail. I always watch the water. Perhaps it's the Viking in me.

Off the ferry, I breathed deep and welcomed myself to south London. I would be working on this side of the river so I might as well start soaking up the atmosphere. It was a lot less Tony Blair down here.

I walked and I soaked. Soon I was in Plumstead without a clue to my name.

I thought I might well benefit from a haircut. I found a barber's with a proper candy-striped pole outside. The barber himself was a neat little man wearing a burgundy coloured coat. He had the appearance of being from Eastern Europe but his accent was sarf laanden.

I waited and read the paper whilst two octogenarian gentlemen took their turn before me. Neither of them had what I would call hair. I watched with fascination as the straight-edged razor dragged the folds of skin at the back of their necks and cleared away a little of the wispy white growth. I had to turn away when they had their nose hairs clipped – especially as the second gent had one of those permanent nasal dewdrops. They both said 'See you next week, Bob' as they left. Their visits were obviously a social ritual rather than anything else.

I asked for a number two. It was as far as I was prepared to go. The electric razor he used seemed almost the size of his forearm. I would have sworn it had a round pin plug too. When he asked the inevitable 'not working today, sir?' I just grunted. But he persisted.

'You ain't local are ya, sir? You on one of them building sites?'

I decided to play along. I was going to

have to start getting into character anyway.

'Work where you can get it, dontcha?' I replied. I would have shrugged but I was paranoid about losing an ear.

'That's about the only work there is round here now. Tearing the old ones down, putting new ones up.'

He sort of nodded towards the shop window. I could indeed see two cranes rising up from behind the other side of the high street.

'Well, it's work.'

I was being a good deal less articulate than normal.

'But not for anyone who lives round here. These builders are from all over the place. No offence to you, sir. I mean, at least you're *English*. I bet you're in a minority working on those sites.'

'Yeah.'

I'd be back to grunting again soon. I decided I would say something.

'But at least when the work's finished – offices, and shops and houses and that – that'll be for the locals, won't it?'

'I suppose so sir,' he replied.

I thought I was being too conciliatory so I added, 'But then who can you call *local* these days? All these immigrants?'

'It's a disgrace sir.'

We did the rest in silence. He slapped his straight-edged razor dramatically back and forth across his leather strap, he splashed the back of my neck and behind my ears with what looked like absinthe, then gave me a blue paper towel to give me something to do with my hands whilst he fumbled in the old wooden cash register for change of a tenner.

I couldn't resist making a guess as I went. 'Bob, are you Ukrainian?'

His face was a picture. I think I had guessed correctly.

He paused, thinking. Then Bob sighed and said, 'I used to be.'

7

As well as a haircut, Bob had also provided me with a suggestion for cover. I began to weave my way through the streets towards the cranes that I could see. Along the way, I rubbed my head and checked my new look in the shop windows. I stopped at a cash machine too. Soon, I found myself walking the length of a substantial wooden construction fence, which offered no reflection. That helped any self-consciousness evaporate, making it easier to approach total strangers as I intended. I suppose the beer was on my side too.

It was around 4.30pm now. It was also a Saturday. I didn't know if the date or time were significant but there seemed to be a steady trickle of workers coming out from the opening of a large mesh gate in the wooden fence.

A group of three men were walking towards me. They were speaking to each other but not in English. They were all dark haired with dark tan skin. Mediterranean?

I tried to get some eye contact and said, 'Excuse me...' But they just kept on walking and talking.

The next likely guy was on his own.

''Scuse me mate...'

He actually stopped. He automatically started fumbling for his lighter.

'What shoe size are you?' I asked innocently.

'Do what?'

'You wouldn't happen to be an eleven, would you?'

He mumbled something uncomplimentary

and walked away.

I ended up loitering at the gate for twenty minutes before I collared a willing participant in my plan.

He was a size ten and a half. It would do.

I offered him a hundred quid for his work boots and jeans. It was enough of a profit margin for him to overcome the psychological weirdness of it all. We swapped right there in the street. The poor guy kept looking round as if he might see a TV camera – or his mum.

I watched him walk away awkwardly wearing my track bottoms and Reeboks. Well, the trainers were about a year and a half old and it would give me the opportunity to buy the New Balance I'd been looking at.

I cast my eyes down at my new gear. The point being that it wasn't new. The boots were scuffed and the jeans were worn. Both were covered in brick dust and flecks of dried cement.

I was in disguise.

At that, I called it a day and made my way back up to Hornsey by combination of train and tube. It was standing room only most of the way and I could feel a subtle difference in the way the public were behaving towards me or, rather, my haircut. It could be the scowl I was practising too. I was going for angry working class white male chic.

I was commanding more physical space than I would normally have done. People who were forced to stand near me seemed to be holding their bodies stiffly as if trying to repel me without actually touching. The exceptions to the rule along the way were two black guys and one black woman who all seemed to militate against my presence by standing as close as they could and getting right in my face. It felt odd. I was pleased for their righteous attitude but I couldn't help feeling a little offended. I took the opportunity to practise more scowling. If the journey had been any longer then maybe one of us would have fainted.

Debs wasn't in when I got back to the house. I went out back to the shed that stood in their thin strip of a garden. None of the other students had been interested in equal shed rights so Debs had cleared it out and hung a heavy bag. I pounded it with combination punches and elbows for about thirty minutes. I kept on my white T-shirt and denim shirt to let them get sweaty. I deliberately didn't wear any mitts in order to raw up my knuckles. They were very red by the time I had finished. So was my face.

Luckily, the house had a working shower. I made excellent use of it. I put on a clean T-shirt and jeans, then set about cooking a meal.

Being a vegan, Debs had a well-stocked larder with all the incidentals you need for proper cooking. Being hard as nails, none of the other students stole food from her. Being a semi-Buddhist, she always cooked enough for everyone. Being a vegan, they rarely ate that shit anyway.

I chopped garlic and ginger. They go in everything. Then green chillies, coriander and onions. They all got wok-fried in vegetable ghee with brown mustard seeds sprinkled in generously. Once the onions had softened I added in a couple of tins of chickpeas and, shortly, some cubed potatoes that had been parboiling whilst I assembled everything else. Then garam masala for flavour, turmeric for colour. Would have loved to have added plain yoghurt and butter but they're animal products so lemon juice and vegetable stock went in instead. The stock was good. Reduced to oblivion from roast veg then frozen – saved from my last visit down. Bit of tomato puree for more colour and richness. Genetically modified, no doubt. Let it bubble whilst I prepared the basmati rice, then chucked some roughly torn coriander on top of the curry. Like lilies on a pond of bubbling clay earth.

Debs came in just then. Perfection.

We ate and told each other about our respective days since parting at Starbucks.

When I got to the bit about my disguise she said, 'Let's see it.'

We went upstairs to her bedroom, where I dutifully pulled on the grubby jeans and boots. Hands on hips, I asked, 'Happy now?'

'Nearly...' she said. Debs picked up a large marker pen from her desk, took the top off with an audible pop, then came over and drew a big swastika on my naked chest – my left pectoral muscle to be exact. It felt wet and cold. Her movements were precise and she had the tip of her tongue ever so slightly protruding from the corner of her lips.

When she'd finished she dropped the pen, ran her fingers through my newly shortened hair – trying to grab what she could of it – pushed her face up close to mine and said, 'Now fuck me, skinhead!'

I threw her onto the bed. It was called for.

I paused and picked up the pen from the floor.

'This gets you hot, yeah?'

She nodded excitedly from her prone

position on the mattress. I dotted a little black Hitler moustache onto my upper lip with the marker, did the seig heil, and jumped on top of her.

Debs was laughing but she made a point of biting into my upper lip and sucking the ink off. Made me wish I'd drawn on some fake pubic hair too.

'And I thought you were going to draw on me...' she said, between our heavy kisses.

'OK' I said, and wrote NIGGA PLEAZ in capital letters across her bare belly. She was quivering. I tucked the pen into my boot – in case I needed it later – then I pulled down my jeans and sank into her.

It was good. Real good. But I can't see us using that particular piece of role-play ever again now.

Sunday morning we ran again then worked out too. We work out well together. I gripped the barbell deliberately tight and felt the calluses forming. I spent much of the rest of the day surfing the internet for background on Combat 18, Blood & Honour, that sort of stuff. The regular search engines didn't help a great deal. You had to start out with the fairly tame right wing sites then just link, link, link until you got to the harder stuff.

I'm no soccer fan, but I thought it might

provide me with something suitable to talk about if I was going to be hanging about in low life boozers, listening for clues. I took in everything I could about Leeds United, whose supporters had *that* kind of reputation – certainly where I came from. I quickly learned that, if you weren't already angry and disaffected before supporting LUFC, then you soon would be.

That night I agreed to let Debra cook, but on the understanding that we could go and get some honeyed pastry desserts from the local Cypriot bakery. She served up peppers stuffed with lentils. Total clash of textures but edible. The pastries were good and I ate some glazed pistachios too as we curled up to watch *True Romance* together. We're so cool.

We slept well.

Monday morning Debs had an early lecture. I tubed it with her to Russell Square and we had espressos and cinnamon toast in a little Italian place. We sat on high chrome seats looking out of the window. The people walking past were well dressed but had bad skin and tired eyes.

I was not well dressed. I had on those jeans and boots. The ensemble was completed with my white T-shirt and light blue denim shirt, both stale with sweat. My knuckles were no longer angry red but were still noticeably fucked. Little shreds of skin were missing and the remaining skin was deliberately dry and dirty, giving the scaly, cracked appearance of chicken feet. I tried not to let my appearance and attire spoil my brief enjoyment of the swanky location.

When it was time for Debra to leave she kissed me tenderly on the forehead. She knew that it was time for me to go to work. She knew not to say, 'What time will you be home tonight?' She understood. She said, instead, 'Take care. Remember you're fighting monsters.'

Then she left.

She was alluding to our mutual favourite philosopher – Friedrich Nietzsche. Nietzsche had once written, *He who fights monsters might take care lest he thereby become a monster. And if you gaze for long into the abyss, the abyss gazes also into you.*

I felt as ready as I'd ever be. I was used to gazing into the abyss. I was fully prepared for the abyss to gaze back. I just wasn't too keen on it nutting me in the face, that's all.

I had a number that Geoffrey Sitcha had given to me. It was for a division of the police called the Community Safety Unit that dealt with 'hate crimes' in the area where he had been attacked. Geoffrey had said they were very polite and sensitive but had made no progress.

I could understand his frustration but I could also see how difficult it was for the law. He hadn't exactly been able to provide any descriptions of his attackers. Also, the same culture of fear and self-preservation that had stopped anyone going to his aid was probably going to make it unlikely that anyone would come forward as a witness after the event for fear of retribution.

Anyway, I phoned the number. I got speaking to a Detective Sergeant Val Townley and she invited me down to the police station at Woolwich for a chat. Painless enough so far.

When I got there I was directed into a medium sized open plan office by one of the uniforms. Val shook my hand and showed me to a seat at her desk whilst she went off to get a couple of coffees. She was a smartly dressed attractive woman in her mid to late thirties. She had sandy coloured hair, freckles and laughter lines. When she got back she handed me the coffee, looked me up and down and said, 'Let me guess. You're in disguise.'

'Busted,' I replied.

'I hope you realise that the "skinhead" look is in decline.'

'I'm playing the part of an ignorant northerner,' I countered.

'Break a leg,' she said dryly.

At my request she filled me in on the work they had done. The ferocity and apparent premeditation of the attack meant they were treating it as attempted murder. Thames-mead CID had handed it over to the Community Safety Unit when Geoffrey had told them he recalled hearing verbal abuse of a racist nature. The use of bleach was also a giveaway. Val told me there had been a spate of racist attacks in which bleach had been used in this way. The attacks had taken place off her patch, somewhere called the Lion Estate in New Cross. She felt this was a different gang who happened to be copying the method.

All the CCTV cameras that might have helped them were already vandalised. They had carried out door-to-door enquiries in the area. This turned up some information but no one was prepared to make a statement. Witness appeal boards had gone up but had been defaced or destroyed. Their unit was obviously professional and dedicated but wasn't, at this point, making any progress. It was all quite depressing.

'What are your intentions, Mr O'Brien?' Val asked me. Very direct.

'It's been informative to know what you've already done. There's no point me trying to duplicate your work – going door to door or anything like that. I'm going to attempt to infiltrate.'

'Really?'

'I thought I might just hear something I could use. These tosspots probably see themselves as hard men. Such people do like to brag.'

She nodded but then said, 'I'd advise extreme caution. These people are not necessarily as easy to out-smart as their politics would indicate. In fact, I'd advise you to head for home and leave this to us.'

'Thought you would,' I shrugged.

'And I can see that you won't,' she smiled.

'But I will be careful.'

We sat in silence for a small while.

'I don't expect you to give me any information,' I said. I inflected the end of the sentence ever so slightly.

'I can't give you any names.'

'Of course not.'

'But if you want to socialise with those of

a racist disposition then I might suggest a pub called The Bucket. It's just off my patch – on the Bexleyheath side of Thamesmead – but it's where they go.'

'Thanks, Val.'

'You'd have found it anyway, a man of your obvious tenacity. I've probably saved you about an hour.'

'I can't wait to get started.'

'Don't get overexcited.'

'Oh, but you see – I like pubs.'

She shook her head.

'You won't like this one.'

8

The Bucket.

I wasn't yet inside but I'd already decided it should be renamed The Toilet. The small tarmac car park at the front of it was separated from the pavement by a low brick wall. I mean low. Three bricks high. In places. The tarmac was home to a white Ford Capri with rusted wheel arches, bald tyres and no tax disc. There was another car, smaller and more box-like. I couldn't tell what make it was because it had been completely burnt out. Charming. What were the chances that indoors they were going to have a ball pool and a kiddie's menu?

The bar was immediately to my right as I walked in and appeared to have no one behind it. The place was dimly lit and fairly empty but the main action was over by the pool table. There was no match on but a group of blokes were gathered around a stocky little pit bull terrier as if it were the new toy in the playground. One of the guys was trying to wrestle a rounders bat away from its growling jaws. A big gob of slaver fell from its flapping black lips and landed on the guy's scuffed Rockports.

I noticed that the carpet had a few burn holes in it. One the size of a small campfire. I noticed various other stains. The people in the bar seemed to notice me in roughly the same way.

I ignored them all and sat myself at the empty bar. Eventually, one of the dog worshippers tore himself away and came around behind the bar to face me.

'What do you want?' he asked.

'To get drunk,' I replied.

He seemed to find that vaguely amusing without actually laughing. I pointed silently at the Fosters tap and he dutifully pulled me a pint. I paid with a twenty. He eyed it for a while, it might be dodgy.

I stayed at the bar, hunching over my pint in a manner that I hoped looked enigmatically dark and brooding. The pool table crowd were glancing over at me every now and then. The cracked strip of mirror behind the optics told me so but it was the kind of hair-on-the-back-of-the-neck-raising attention you could sense anyway. A few of the optics were empty. All were dust-covered. There was no Bacardi. No Tia Maria, Baileys or Aftershock. This was not somewhere you took a lady.

The barman was back over there with the lads, so when I finished my pint I put the empty down on the bar and walked over.

'Same again when you're ready, mate, and does anyone want a game?'

'If you're payin',' said one of them. He had a yellow Lambretta T-shirt and a prominent glassing scar just above his jawbone. I think he was the leader of that particular pack, though he had a vulnerable quality to him. Wasn't able to hold my gaze for long.

'Long as you keep that dog from shaggin' me leg – game's on me.'

'She's well behaved,' he said with some pride.

'Not trained to kill me if I win, I hope.'

He laughed at that. Seemed to like the idea.

'Anyway, mate,' I added, 'I'll tell you now – I'll probably lose anyway. I'm shit at pool. Just fancy a game.'

'And I'll tell *you* now – if you're on the con you can forget it. I ain't got no money to put down.'

'No really. I am shit.'

So we started playing. I had a pint brought over to me and I stood my opponent one too. We got chatting. His name was John. He and his mates were all skint. Monday lunchtime. Giro wasn't until Tuesday. The Bucket let them run a limited tab.

As we racked up for a second game – I'd lost the first – I offered to get the rest of them a pint. There were only five of them after all. With their drinks, they started to gather round John and me a little more. I'd say they were grateful but suspicious.

'I've worked hard for my wage, I deserve a few drinks, and – finally – I've found some good fucking company!' I pronounced.

I told them that I'd been working on a building site. I told them it was 'by the flyover' and gestured wildly with my arm, pretending to be a little more drunk than I was. Told them I'd been forced to work with a bunch of Turks, Gypo's and Pakis all week until I'd finally twatted one of them and got booted off the site. I got into a bit of a rant. I said I was used to Pakis cooking my curries and driving my taxis Up North but I'd always considered the building trade to be 'white man's work'.

They listened eagerly as I told them about my antics so far over the weekend – all the pubs I'd been chucked out of and that. I said that what was pissing me off about London was that you couldn't avoid fucking foreigners wherever you went.

John totally agreed. Told me that, if he could ever raise the money, he was moving to Essex. Then he asked how I'd managed to find this place.

'A policewoman told me,' I said truthfully.

I explained that, at the last place I was being chucked out of for racial abuse, one of the filth suggested I might fit in well at a shit-hole called The Bucket. Even gave me directions.

God forgive me if they didn't all cheer at that. Pride's a funny thing.

'You here to spend all your hard-earned then?' asked John.

'When I head back home early, the missus

is gonna go ape anyway – might as well go for broke.'

The crowd nodded and murmured their approval at my cavalier attitude – especially when I went ahead and bought them another round. I was one of the lads now, with my finger on the pulse of their priorities. Life was about looking after yourself and then your mates. Living for the moment because the future was too bleak to contemplate. Living from giro to giro, fix to fix, pint to pint, cig to cig, and – from the look of those enlarged knuckles and scar-pitted faces – fight to fight. A desperate existence.

But something about it was seductive – perhaps its very simplicity.

I was quite enjoying myself to be honest and I had to guard against it. Take this 'method acting' too far and I'd end up dead – or at least dead drunk. I had to keep my focus.

I was doing a couple of active daoist meditations, not so as you'd notice – just kept tuning into them every now and then. One was my *Cosmic Egg*. I visualise, as a kind of radiance, an oval of energy around me. It protected my consciousness from being invaded by the negative energies of my companions. It also projected confidence and charisma. Made people want to like me. So I told myself anyway.

The other exercise was basically another visualisation but this time of energy flowing through my body in a repetitive loop. Kept me physically and mentally alert – ready for action – and, I like to think, detoxified my beer-soaked circulation.

It's probably a dangerous delusion, but I reckon I've built up a kind of beer immunity. I can drink the stuff all day and still function. Years of practise.

The 'all day' bit is relevant too. Hit the pubs after work and cram it all in before closing time and you *will* get pissed. Our digestive and transformative energies are not geared up to evening activity. Ask an acupuncturist.

Evening came around and the crowd had grown in dribs and drabs. The dog was asleep under a table now – one of its back legs dream-kicking every so often. I'd moved onto mixing rather than holding court. There were no formal introductions. I'd see people checking me out as they came in. They'd make discreet mouth to ear enquiries of whoever was around them. Then they would look at me again, wait for eye contact, and give a brief nod. A gesture of acceptance.

The atmosphere changed noticeably when a geezer and two of his mates walked in. That's the way it was. Not three guys walking in together. A dignitary and two lackeys. You could tell. The camaraderie in the room turned up a notch, but so did the apprehension. Fear, even.

This was Malc. Malc Harper. I'd been told about him earlier and I was now putting two and two together. He was the spiritual leader of this lot. He didn't have a job either. Not one with a pension scheme and six monthly appraisals anyway. He collected the odd debt here and there. He never paid for anything at The Bucket because he was responsible for making sure everyone else paid for theirs.

I had been warned that, if I spoke to him, I should only call him Malc. He didn't like his real name. It was made deadly clear to me that if I made the mistake of saying 'Malcolm' then it would be the last word I'd ever speak.

He was my height. A straight six foot. He looked wider than me but that could have been his puffa jacket. His face was wide though. Steroids maybe. He had a blond flat top that made him look a little like Barney Rubble but without the benign smile. He looked mean. Sadistic. It was in his eyes. But not mean and stupid. There was intelligence in there too. That made him really scary. A piercing analytical gaze that seemed to come from the inside of his head and out through his eyes – scanning for potential threats, potential victims.

That 'Terminator' gaze was on me straight away. He also seemed to know somehow that John had taken me under his wing, as it was him who was approached for the whisper. I could see John's body tense. He leant in to Malc's lips, awkwardly offering himself – like he was scared that his ear might get bitten off if he did, but like something even worse might happen if he didn't.

I didn't get a nod of acceptance from Malc. He and his two mates just turned and went to the bar. I tried not to take offence. I suppose the fact that I hadn't been immediately identified as an outsider and shown the door was acceptance enough.

I went for another drink. It had been busy enough for a while now and the barman was no longer hanging out with the lads.

'Same again, Al, and one each for these guys if they want one.'

Malc and his mates heard my unfamiliar northern accent behind them, my voice slightly louder than it should have been from beer and nerves, and turned to face me.

Malc looked me slowly up and down before saying a word. I could tell the other two were up for the offer of a drink but they weren't going to speak before he did.

'Cheers. We'll have one. So, Chris is it?'

'Yup. That's me. I'm Chris. Pleased to meet you Malcolm...'

9

It was a good punch. Malc snapped it out really quickly but still managed to put some shoulder into it. If I didn't make it my business to take a good punch once in a while then he'd probably have sparked me.

I had set myself up for it. Knew it was coming. I'd deliberately wandered into punching range just as the perceived insult was delivered – making it his most likely form of instant retribution. I hadn't dodged it at all. I'd even leaned into it a little so that it didn't reach full velocity. We martial artists call it a 'destruction' – a counter move that takes the force out of an attack. Normally you wouldn't use your face. Just on the point of impact I'd then rolled my head up and away to the side, taking even more force away from the blow but adding some drama too. All timed to perfection.

Then I fell on me arse. That was the easy part. Like I say, it was a good punch. I'm not sure I could have stayed on my feet if I'd wanted to.

Once down there, I held my jaw and performed a sort of comedy jiggle of my head. Muttered a couple of under-the breath obscenities then looked up at Malc and said,

'Oh aye. Remember now. Malc in't it? Fucking good punch, Malc,' I said with a drunken grin.

I had one eye on my path to the door, in case my clowning wasn't enough and it all kicked off. Plan was I'd roll to my feet and trust the Dao to pick me up and carry me. Feets don't fail me now.

But it worked. A ripple of laughter went round the room. Malc remained stony-faced but motionless. Main thing was that he wasn't leaping all over me. I was still on the floor – like a dog displaying its defeated belly. Malc had saved face almost the instant he'd lost it. He'd reinforced his image to those around him. He had nothing else to prove right now. He was still The Man.

Only I was too. I'd dissed him to his face. I guess no one had seen that done for a while. I'd taken a dig but I was still smiling – if not standing. I had respect. Add to that the amount of drinks I'd been shelling out for. I was the next man.

Maybe there were other factors at work. Sometimes, if loyalty is motivated only by fear, people are just waiting for an uprising. Maybe Malc knew that as he stood there, with a smarting fist looking down at a potential opponent who was neither unconscious nor cowering. Maybe he was wondering what would happen if everyone stepped back and gave us a square go.

I started slowly to my feet. Still ready for booted feet to lash out at me. For a second I thought of Geoffrey Sitcha and my blood ran cold with my own vulnerability. Then the spark of anger was there and my blood ran hot – remembering why I was doing this. Why I was prepared to take this risk.

But Malc nodded to Al behind the bar and said, 'He's payin',' then turned his back on me.

There was hearty, good-natured laughter

all around. People seemed to like me. I was *one of them*. I was relieved, but I couldn't help feeling a little unclean.

For the rest of the evening, my blood ran beer.

Luckily, no one talked too much about football. The meagre research I'd done wouldn't have stood up to a great deal of scrutiny. Violence was the main topic of conversation. That suited me. I'm not a violent man but I do work the door of a nightclub on occasions and I'd seen some action and heard plenty of stories. Normally told with more circumspection and less relish than I was hearing at the moment.

Anyway, with all that to draw upon I became quite the storyteller. I adapted, I embellished, I added more than a dash of racism. I was Joe Pesci in *Goodfellas*. I had an audience.

Even Malc was listening. He was on the edge of the group. He wasn't nodding along with enthusiasm but he was there. I was starting to hog the limelight. *His* limelight. They'd heard all his stories before. I bet he was wishing he'd done me over when he'd had the chance.

'You're quite the hard man aren't you, Chris?' Malc said when my audience went quiet. The audience stayed quiet. There was a challenge in the question.

'Nowt like you, Malc. Jaw's still stiff as fuck.'

'You seem to be using it okay.' Laughs all round. Dig at me. Everyone starting to remember who's really top man around here.

'Just enjoying the company, mate.'

'All these kickings you've handed out – you ever kill anyone?'

'I don't make a point of phoning the hospitals afterward to check. How should I fuckin' know?' I'm a cocky little git.

'I think you'd know. Kill a nigger or a paki and it's all over the news for the next couple of years. Makes you sick. Who was the last white person to die they made a fucking fuss of?'

'Princess Diana?'

'You're a right comedian, aren't you?'

'No, you're right, Malc. I'm sick of hearing about Stephen-fucking-Lawrence and Danny-fucking-Taylor-wotsit. Fuck 'em. Fuck the lot of 'em.' I raised my glass to my lips, dramatically downed the rest of my pint, slammed the empty down, and said, 'Kill 'em all.'

'I think we're all with you on that,' smiled Malc.

'*You* ever kill anyone?' I turned the question back to him.

'We're working on it,' he said.

'If I happen to be around – count me in.'

'Keep drinking, keep talking. I haven't sussed you out yet.'

I nodded and went for a much-needed piss. Praying to God he didn't suss a thing.

Well after closing time and I was back at the pool table. I could see at least two of every ball and the edges of my vision were swimming. Red and yellow blobs danced on a landscape of vivid green. It made me think of the Tellytubbies. The air around me felt thick.

We were now down to a hard core of eight lads, if you included me and Al the barman. There was Malc and his two mates Kev and Russ – who both suffered from a bad case of bodybuilder's arse – there was John, who'd taken his dog home at around eight o'clock but had come back to join us with ketchup all down his Lambretta t-shirt, there was Eddo – who had an interesting skin complaint – and then there was Damian, who was without the benefit of two front teeth.

We few, we happy few.

These were not young lads either. Mid to late twenties at least. To me they seemed older. Popular culture had turned these guys into dinosaurs. Most working class, inner city teenagers spoke and dressed like they wanted to be black. Even the Asian youth did the same. Gangsta rap and gang culture had been around and been growing for some time. Now, with Marshall Mathers bringing his brand of white trash angst to the party, it was deeply unfashionable to talk of niggers. Unless you put an A on the end. You could discharge your pissed-offness by fighting a rival gang, regardless of their colour. Non-discriminatory violence. Racism itself had become unfashionable. Sexism and homophobia, however, were the new black.

But these guys – these dinosaurs – didn't have any rivals. They were top of the food chain in their local community and like hell were they gonna listen to Tim Westwood or try and talk like Ali G.

Malc came over to me and leaned towards my ear. His breathing was rapid and moist, his eyes flickered, his face was hot. I think he'd necked some whizz.

'OK Chris. Are you up for some action then?'

'Thought you'd never ask. We off paki bashing are we?'

'Even better. You ever raped a black girl?'

I shook my head. I couldn't help myself. It was the kind of shake where you don't like what you're hearing and you're denying the reality of it.

But Malc just took it as a 'No.'

'Well, tonight's your lucky night, boy!'

10

The girl paced the cold pavement. The streetlights hummed a blur of orange haze that stole magic from the night. A question was echoing through the thoughts she carried with her.

Why do you do it? That was what they all asked. With a furrowed brow and a sense of great importance. Like a theologian asking, *'Why does God allow suffering?'* Only there was always an accusation in there too, with a sense that you had let everybody down. Like an interviewer asking a politician *'Why did you lie to the people?'* Then they always managed to cram exasperation and impatience into that little question. Parent to child – *'Why did you spill juice on the carpet...again?'*

Answer it yourself. You're supposed to be the fucking expert.

All right, I'll tell you. But I'm no expert either. I can only tell you about me, and I'm not even sure I know who I am anymore anyway.

Why do you do it? I do it because I want to wake up. It's the worst kind of nightmare. The world looks like the same sort of place but it's different. People I know are still here but they treat me differently. They speak to me differently. Everything I say comes out sounding weird. Everything I do is wrong.

So I pinch myself. I don't wake up. I scratch myself. I don't wake up. I bite myself. I don't wake up. I take a razor and I cut myself. I don't wake up. They take the razor off me and say, *'Why do you do it?'* They give me something to make me sleep. Sometimes it works. I sleep. I wake up. But *still* I don't wake up. I find some glass, tear up a Coke can, whatever, and I cut myself. I don't wake up.

I cut deeper and deeper, hoping I'll wake up. I know the danger. I know that I might die if I cut myself too bad. But if you're dead you don't wake up. So what's the difference? Maybe I'm dead already.

I don't want to die. Listen to me. I don't want to die. I mean it. I don't want to die. But I don't want *this* life.

I don't want to die. I don't really want to hurt myself at all. But I want other people to stop hurting me. If I was dead they couldn't touch me.

Why do you do it? What would Chris O'Brien say? I know. He'd say, 'Maybe you want someone to love you enough to stop you.'

That's right. Stop me somebody. Love me enough. The Prince kisses Sleeping Beauty. She wakes up.

Stop me somebody.

The girl walked silently on. The soles of her bare feet stinging as they slapped stone. Fresh blood from deep gashes on her forearms soaking down to the cuffs of her baggy sweatshirt. Cotton sticking awkwardly and dragging at the wet scabs of the older wounds. She stared into the eyes of every passer-by, looking for love.

Plenty of people who were near the railway bridge that night hurried past that scruffy girl with the mad eyes.

Would anyone stop her?

11

My heart was thumping. My vision cleared a little. Rather than fight the wave of nausea and adrenaline I thought I'd better ride it. Make it look like I was excited, aroused. Not ready to burst with anger or collapse with fear.

I gulped, and then spoke.

'Shit. Yeah. I'll have some of that. You got anyone in mind?'

Trying to gather what information I could about what I was getting myself into.

'No. Just some whore. There's a street in Lewisham we can pick one up. Eddo will drive us all over.'

More information than I'd hoped for in just one sentence. Eddo was the owner of a battered red transit that had pulled up earlier. I forced my face into a lascivious grin.

'Maybe we'll get to fuck a pimp while we're at it.'

'Chris, you catch on quick.'

In a display of wanton ignorance, I pulled my mobile from its resting place on my hip and started to make a call.

'WHAT THE FUCK ARE YOU PLAY-ING AT?' Malc bellowed at me as he snatched the Nokia 7110 from my hand and rammed his body into mine, leaning me on the pool table and spitting frothy rage into my face. Everyone was looking at us.

I gave him innocent.

'This mate I'm staying with in Deptford ... he'll want in on this.'

'For fuck's sake!' he ranted. 'Think yourself fucking lucky we're letting you ride with us. This is serious. You're recruited. You're ours. This is your initiation. You can't back out now and you can't phone a fucking friend!'

They all stared at me like I'd crapped in their coffee.

'Malc?'

'What?'

'Can I ask the audience?'

That got a laugh. Even from him.

'The audience says – one more drink and we're off,' retorted Eddo, having trouble with the S's on either side of the word 'says'.

That's something, I thought. Maybe we'll all crash and die and I won't have to go through with this.

'Well, I'm off for a slash. Want my tackle in

working order, don't I?'

I hated the sound of my voice as I said it. I hated the sound of their joyless laughter even more. Malc held my phone up.

'I'll hang on to this for you. Don't want you calling your mum to come and pick you up 'cos you've changed your mind.'

I shrugged like it wasn't a problem.

'Don't be using up my credit while I'm gone.' I wagged my finger at him and departed for the bogs.

They weren't going to find anything incriminating in the messages or the phone book. I'd made sure of that before I came out. I hadn't bought a wallet or any ID with me either.

The 'gentlemen's' – if it could be called that – had one cubicle with a cracked toilet bowl and badly mis-spelt graffiti, an old style porcelain urinal trough with standing space for three, and one sink with a cold water tap. Not a soap dispenser in sight. Earlier on, at the height of its activity, the sink had become the favoured urinal when a floating dam of soggy cigarette ends slowed the drainage of communal piss until it swelled to Yangztse Kiang proportions and started lapping onto the toes of many a pair of Kappa trainers.

The place was empty now, giving the piss a chance to slowly gurgle and subside. There was one of those oblong metal boxes attached to the wall, a navy blue piece of cloth hanging almost redundantly from the slot at the bottom. I snaked my hand up inside and retrieved my back-up mobile, which I'd hidden there earlier in the evening before the bogs got busy. It was stuck halfway up the inside by a strip of double-sided sticky.

The Ericsson T28 may not be the most compact handset on the market these days, maybe not even the lightest, but it's got to be the thinnest. You could hide it in the mortar between two bricks. Unnoticeable in the pocket of your Levis. Less bulky than one of those flippy chrome affairs. Powerful aerial too.

I'd just performed a classic 'give-away'. Allowed Malc to feel he had control over me now. Possession of my Nokia was a kind of symbolic removal of my power. Communicational castration.

But what exactly was I going to do? I couldn't very well call the police and begin calmly explaining the situation to a civilian switchboard operator. I had to make seconds count.

So I did what any bloke in a dangerous, violent, potentially life-threatening situation would do.

I called my girlfriend for help.

Well, I texted.

6 drunk nazis plan 2 rape blk grl 2nite in lwshm. In red transit. Get help.

There was an unspoken knowledge that she would be ready and waiting for any contact from me. Not worrying. Not watching the clock for me to finish working and come home. Just ready. Debra was, quite simply, ready for action at all times. If you ever meet someone like that, the first thing you'll notice is how calm they are. They are conserving energy – containing it. Prepared to do whatever the situation requires at a moment's notice. Being a few miles across London, knowing roughly what I was getting myself into, and because she'd sort of got me into it, she was *involved*.

So I could depend on her to summon some help on my behalf. Pity I also had to depend on the vagaries of satellite positioning.

Back in the bar, the lads were having just one more for the road. Opaque silver bottles of vodka-laced stimulant drink seemed to be doing the rounds. It was the place's only concession to modernity.

Malc had obviously located the little button that released the sliding cover on my mobile and was sat there amusing himself with it. I held my hand out and after a long pause that I suppose was intended to wind me up he handed it back.

'Just like in *The Matrix*, eh?' he said.

I just nodded, having to consciously stop myself from saying, 'I know Kung Fu' – like the sad fan-boy that I am.

I prayed for them all to drink slowly, to give Debs time to get a police presence into the red light area of Lewisham by fair means or foul. I started on a bottle myself, hoping to make it last, but anxiety was making my mouth so dry that I was chugging at it before I realised. Great. More alcohol. I mentally kicked myself for not being focused. Was I up to any of this?

Too late for soul searching as Eddo lead us out across the uneven surface of the potholed car park to our dark and dented chariot. It looked unsightly and foreboding – as if it had been designed as a weapon of choice for aggressive drivers and child molesters. I wondered if this might well have been the vehicle that Geoffrey Sitcha managed to roll clear of. I thought too of the anonymous van that my mate Kelp had been hauled into and beaten near to death last autumn. *Transport from Hell.*

There were no windows in the back and it stank of sour milk and perished rubber. It sounded like it was dragging a sack of spanners behind it. Eddo drove, Malc and Key sat up front with him. We all crammed up against the back of the seats behind them, craning our necks to watch the black road lit with patches of orange roll towards us through the windshield. Light from petrol stations and all night minimarts dotted the nocturnal streets at randomly spaced intervals, like teeth in a smashed mouth. It was either look out of the window or look at each other's ugly mugs, twisted with hate and hunger. At one point we pulled over below a railway arch and Eddo got out a set of bogus plates. He secured them over the genuine plates with large crocodile clips. He'd done this before. It didn't take long but I was glad of any delay, as it would give more time for Debs to get some sort of response together. The best I could really hope for was that the lads would just see too many police on the street and give it up as a bad job.

Give it up for that night at least. What

about the next time? What should I do about that? What *could* I do about that? Or about any number of thugs, crims, nutters and terrorists who were at this very moment plotting harm against their fellow man?

Big questions. Good job I'd done philosophy at Uni. It was all about facing difficult questions that had no conventionally right or wrong answers. It was about seeking Truth. It was *Investigation*. But the career progression towards sitting in a metal box with a gang of thugs intent on hate crimes had never been mentioned by any of my tutors.

No, the best wisdom had come straight from the detective novels I had read. From my old favourite Spenser – 'You can't always do what you should – sometimes you have to settle for doing what you can.'

I hoped that what I could do was going to be good enough.

Eventually, the van slowing down to cruising speed and the way Malc was leaning forward slightly in his seat – like a hunting dog catching a scent – told me that we were there.

It wasn't the town centre but it wasn't quite suburbia either. It was a wide street with occasional trees and one prominent zebra crossing that reminded me of Abbey

Road. Or of the album cover at least, as I'd never actually been there. The housing let it down. Squat flats and maisonettes set a little way back from the pavement. No gardens, just treasured parking spaces. There were also a couple of factories, a college building and a bus depot closed for the night.

No police anywhere. Not good.

The girls were there though. Working in groups of two or three. Wearing very little and wearing it badly. They all appeared to be of Afro-Caribbean descent.

We parked the van up in a side street and waited for a while. Malc explained that we were waiting to get just one girl on her own. They didn't like to work the street alone but sooner or later, when the punters were busy enough, the girls ended up with no choice but to brazen it out whilst their mates were off on other jobs. He said they'd done this before but they always chose different areas. He said the rapes hadn't been reported. He thought this was due to a combination of shame and lack of faith in the police. It was all I could do not to kill him there and then.

We sat with the engine idling for a while until Malc gave the nod that it was time for another look. We pulled out of the side street and back up the main drag, cruising past the groups of girls we had seen before. They stared at us as we crept past, their faces a mixture of hardness and helplessness. They didn't trust the van. Good for them. It was hardly the mode of transport for an unhappy businessman looking for what he couldn't get at home.

But as we neared the other end of the street, Malc leaned forward a little and my heart sank in time. He had spotted his prey.

A lone girl coming into view. Her long, dark, straight hair scraped back tight against her skull, weighted down with gel that glinted in the streetlight. She wore white high-top sneakers and black Lycra cycling shorts. A black and red bustier cinched in her waist and drew the eyes up towards her prominent breasts.

It was a nice bustier. I should know. I bought it for her.

It was Debra Prentice.

Jesus H Christ.

12

Jesus, Mary and Joseph. I should have known. I could just imagine her now, getting the text. Rape a black girl? They can try this one. Six of them? A threat. They were drunk, gave her an edge. She had the element of surprise, gave her a major edge. Add in a drunk O'Brien as back-up and the threat might begin to look like an enjoyable challenge to her.

No. She wasn't that daft. What was she playing at?

I was twitching and trembling as the van pulled up beside her. Spasms running up and down the length of my back and into my shoulders. Arsehole felt like the Grand Canyon. Eddo kept the engine running. Malc turned to us lads in the back and grinned. Then he looked at me and spoke.

'Kev'll go out and "speak" to her. He likes to get the first shot in. As soon as he hits or grabs her, the rest of us drag her into the back.'

I nodded. I wanted to destroy him, but I

just nodded.

Key stepped out of the van. As soon as he did, I was clambering over the front seat.

'What you doing?' snapped Malc.

'1 want to watch,' I said with some force. Malc let it go unchallenged and then there I was – sat next to him and peering across out of the passenger window. We had the window cracked a little so we could hear. Kev did his bodybuilder's waddle over to my girl. My girl was looking stunning, I must add. Because I knew what to look for, I could see her shifting slightly so that she was just beyond arms length. If he crossed the battle line she had set up in front of her, it would act as a trigger for immediate action. She looked relaxed though – her body loose and ready to move.

'How much?' he asked. Smooth-talking bastard, that Kev.

Debs, hands on hips, looked quickly down at herself and then straight back into Kev's face.

'Don't think you can afford *this*.'

He didn't reply to that. I fancy he made a movement with his nostrils but I couldn't actually see his face. Debs continued. 'Standard rate. But there gonna be a surcharge for your level of extreme ugliness.'

'How much we talking?' I think Kev was too dense to appreciate the insult.

'One hundred thousand million billion quid.'

Kev was obviously sick of talking. It was the most I'd heard him say all night. Violence is what happens when you run out of words. Kev must have lived in a world full of violence, but as he stepped into Debra's space it was about to get full to bursting.

His left hand went to her right shoulder, like he was going to hold her in place and thump her with his right. She immediately grabbed it with her right hand and trapped it to her as she pivoted backwards, using the momentum of his arm going forward to pull him off balance. Almost simultaneously her left arm was swiping into action – flying over his left arm, smashing it down in a stiff clubbing motion yet turning suddenly flexible and swooping up again from under it for her left hand to grab at his throat. In that one movement she had his left arm first deadened numb then pinned and wrapped up like a pretzel. It would snap like one too if he moved in any other direction than where she wanted him to. Down was the only way he was going.

The trap with the right hand had only

been a split second thing to position the guy. As soon as her left hand was at his windpipe her right hand became a claw to his face.

It was a *Shaolin Tiger* move. I'd shown it to her a few weeks ago. I'd only ever done it in slow motion myself. She'd shown me a leg sweep in return, which I'm still working on and still not getting right.

The claw hand can do real damage or it can hurt just enough to scare the hell out of you. Whichever option she'd gone for, it caused big Kev to scream like a tiny infant. This had all happened mighty quick and the lads in the back Russ, John and Damian – had barely worked out that something was amiss. They had been waiting for a scream to galvanise them into action so they were all bundling out of the back doors now. I think they had been expecting a female scream though and there was a sense of confusion to their movements.

I had to act. I was hemmed in between Malc and Eddo and staring out the fucking window whilst it was all kicking off. Malc made a move and decided it for me. He flung open the passenger door. I elbowed Eddo in the temple, rolling my forearm across the back of his head out of the same movement then pushed downwards and smashed his psoriasis scarred face into the steering wheel. I was out of the door too and on Malc's back the moment he was on the street. I took him hard to the floor with a jarring thud that made me think of playgrounds, grazed knees and British Bulldog. The scuffle began. His initial surprise counted for shit all. It was a terrible thing to do. I was now rolling around on the pavement arena with the taste of sick in my throat, leaving Debs to face the other three.

Malc was not happy with the traitor in his midst. He was thrashing about wildly, a big battling ball of muscle with spikes sticking out of it, smothering me. He wanted to kill me. He was probably going to.

That's always been my problem in a fight. Zero killer instinct. Too civilized. All I ever want to do is express my displeasure. There's a big difference between wanting to kill your opponent and wanting to tell them off. Oh, and I always want to win too. But then I'd be happy to be friends afterwards. This was no playground.

I'd managed to notice that John was on the floor in front of Debs. A crumpled heap of wounded bollocks. Kev was back up again though. Although his left arm was hanging useless you had to give him credit for being on his feet. Debs doesn't normally let that happen. Russ and Damian were closing on her and suddenly I wasn't paying attention to my own fight anymore. My vision going bright in the darkness, the taste of blood and snot in my mouth, only barely feeling the punches that were raining down on me. A strange cold feeling down the back of my neck, and Debra yelling my name. Malc saying, 'You fucking know each other?' from somewhere above me. Debra grunting in pain. Eddo out of the van now shouting, 'Hold him for me!'

Blood in my eyes.

Then the pop and shatter of broken glass. Then the loud loud boom of something heavy on resonant metal. The violence freeze-framed.

Geoffrey Sitcha standing tall and proud on the roof of Eddo's transit. Pickaxe handle gripped loosely but firmly in each hand. Baggy white trousers like a *capoeirista*, bare to the waist and scary as fuck. Muscles working under obsidian skin blacker than the night around him. He seemed to absorb the light.

Then he leapt, whirled, and as his bare feet were hitting the ground so were the bodies of two nazi opponents. Felled like blades of grass.

It was kind of inspiring. I somehow found the strength to plant my foot, raise my knee and roll Malc to the side of me, my right hand chopping at his throat as I did so. That bought Eddo into view and I drove my left fist into his lobster red forehead – right where a bruise from the steering wheel was forming. He was ready to give up there and then but Geoffrey made sure of Eddo's continued non-involvement by smashing one of his sticks into the back of his thighs.

Debs had Malc by now, and she was welcome to him. Reverse hammer fist into his steroid shrivelled groin. Several times. She then barged at his chest with her shoulder, sending him a couple of staggering steps to the side. This may well have been for Geoffrey's benefit, as his two sticks clattered to the pavement and he launched into the air. A flying sidekick that was probably meant to take Malc's head clean off. Placement slightly off. Think he probably only broke his neck.

The nazis were all lying vanquished on the ground. Geoffrey and Debs were standing. I was kneeling. That make us the winners.

'That one,' said Geoffrey, pointing at

Malc, who was still conscious but wheezing and coughing foamy blood, 'I recognised his voice.'

'His name's Malcolm,' I said helpfully.

Geoffrey bent over to speak into his ear.

'Pleased to meet you again, Malcolm.'

Do you know, Geoffrey Sitcha didn't get punched at all?

13

Debra and Geoffrey helped me to my feet.

'How do you feel?' asked Debs.

I coughed a little before replying. Wiped some blood from my chin with the back of my hand.

'How would you feel if you'd just been rescued by MC Hammer and one of his dance crew?'

She smiled but was still serious.

'You annoyed at me, OB?'

'Darling, not in front of the Nazis.' I indicated our battered foes with a sweep of my hand. 'Let's go somewhere and discuss what just happened.'

'Where you thinking? All night bar?

Casualty department?'

'Your place or Geoffrey's, whichever's nearest.'

We made to walk off but a mournful groan from Damian paused us. He was trying to roll from a side-on foetal position to a half sitting position, without actually moving either of his hands that were cradling his skull. One of his moves was too sudden – he retched and vomited bile, with perhaps a few fragment of tooth and kebab thrown in.

'For fuck's sake,' he said in a wet whisper, with a slight whistle caused by his gap tooth, 'Call me an ambulance.'

Geoffrey Sitcha grinned wide and replied, 'You, my friend, are an ambulance.'

We went to Geoffrey's place in St. John's Wood. He drove us there in a metallic blue VW Golf with one of those new number plates. It was a small flat but had nice things in it. He told me his father was a banker. He opened a small combination safe set into the wall behind a decorative leather shield and took out two rolls of notes.

'You work very quickly, O'Brien,' he said. 'Two days work. I will pay you five hundred a day...'

He threw me a roll that I presume was a

grand. Then he started peeling off some more notes.

'...and for the violence you suffered, I think another £500.'

'I do have a fee structure, Geoffrey.'

'Isn't this more than you would normally earn?'

'Yes, but...'

'And expenses? Please list them.' Peeling off more notes as he spoke. I drew breath.

'Jeans and boots: £100. Beer: £150. Haircut: £4.50. Being condescended to: Priceless.'

'I'm sorry?'

'Geoff, you're a nice guy. I'm glad to have helped you. It's just that, as soon as it came to the money, well, I don't know, you're managing to make me feel small.'

His face fell. He looked hurt. I felt even smaller.

'I want to reward you,' he said plaintively.

'No need. Just pay me. Maybe say "Thanks" if you want.' Debra was looking relaxed and amused. She sat expansively on a luxurious two-seater, her arms spread either side of her on the back rest, her chocolate thighs scissoring against each other.

'Just call it two grand. And if there's a £500 going for the violence, then I want it too,' she said coolly.

Geoffrey seemed more comfortable with her businesslike approach. He handed me the second grand roll and went back to the safe for another £500 for Debs, which he pressed into her palm almost ceremoniously. He was silent throughout but then turned to me and said, 'Thank you very much for helping me. I am deeply sorry for being condescending.'

'Geoffrey, easy now. You managed not to shove those notes down Debra's top – we're cool.'

We all laughed. It hurt my jaw a little. Geoffrey fixed me and him some excellent cognac whilst Debs drank some sort of hippy fruit cordial from a tall thin bottle. She was looking at me expectantly, waiting for me. I sighed, and then spoke.

'I feel like I've been used.'

'Is that what you *think* happened?' asked Debs.

'No. How could any of us know how it would turn out? I wasn't following anyone's instructions. I wasn't lied to. No, I don't think either of you used me.'

'But you still *feel* that way...'

'Yes.'

Geoffrey was sitting and listening. He

could see that this was purely between me and Debs.

'You had to pretend that you were something you're not. It's emotionally draining. That's what you feel, OB. All the chocolate's been eaten and now you're just an empty wrapper.

'Cheers, Oprah.'

'You know it's true, babe. Why do we do what we do? Why don't we wear suits and work the nine to five?'

'Because we can't be what we're not.'

'Right. I was a good soldier. You were a good nurse. We were capable of giving heart and soul. But we weren't nobody's *employees*. It's gotta be more than just a job.'

'Agreed. But I'm a PI now. I'm always pretending to be someone I'm not. Always some pretext, some scam.'

'But that's who you are. Using your brain, getting the best result, bending the rules if you have to, blurring the boundaries when the boundaries become barriers.'

'Stunning alliteration.'

'I'm quoting you, babe.'

She was too.

'What happened tonight was you let those boundaries blur too much,' Debra continued. 'You swallowed too much nastiness and now it tastes real bad. Just bring yourself back. Sip your exquisite fire water and chill.'

She was right. I'd let my *Cosmic Egg* lapse too soon. I'd become immersed in bad lager, bad lighting, and bad feeling. I savoured the cognac; let my eyes linger on some of the artwork adorning the walls and furniture of Geoffrey's place. Tried to bring myself back into world of finer things. Perhaps I'd ask him to put the radio on so I could listen to the World Service.

'Anyway,' added Debs, 'your methods certainly got a result.'

'That's what bugging me too, I suppose.' I turned to Geoffrey, 'You consider the job done then?'

'You knew I wanted revenge,' he said without guilt.

'But was it Justice?'

'It wasn't due process of the law,' he agreed, 'but can you call that Justice either?'

'All right. I can see how you might want them to suffer a kicking. But don't you want to put them away? Stop them from doing the same to others?'

'Maybe they will be deterred now from attacking others.'

'Maybe. Maybe not.'

Geoffrey shrugged and sipped his drink.

'Did you expect it to happen like it did?'

'I did not know what to expect. But Debra told me to be ready.'

I looked round at her.

'I had a pretty good idea it would turn out like it did,' she admitted.

'Well how? I went out there without a clue.'

'That's you, honey,' she smiled, 'and I know you. I know what your skills are. You can walk into a crowd of strangers and make them want to like you. I knew you'd just go looking to befriend those losers and that you'd do it. Reckoned it was a safe bet they'd want to impress their new friend by putting on a show. We were just waiting in the wings.'

'What if it had been a completely different set of tossers, not the ones who attacked Geoffrey?'

'We still get to kick ass, and enjoy it.'

'This is getting dangerously close to the "I feel used" conversation.'

'Did you do anything here that wasn't completely your own choice?'

'No.'

'Did you get killed?'

'No.'

'Then, OB, have a Coke and a smile and

shut the fuck up.'

I smiled. I was still sulking a tiny bit on the inside, but Debra mainly makes me smile.

We sat in silence for a while. Nursing our drinks and our wounds. An antique mahogany Grandfather chimed 3.00am. Geoffrey spoke.

'What you were saying earlier, about being what you are. It interests me. It ought to be the simplest thing – to be what you are. But it is so difficult.'

'Maybe impossible,' I said. 'Unattainable Being. Me and Debs tend to agree that we spend our whole lives *becoming* what we are.'

'*Ecce Homo*,' intoned Debs. Nietzsche again.

'And most people spend most of their time *avoiding* becoming. Looking for answers outside of themselves – in a religion, a relationship, a bottle.'

'I strive to be autonomous, self-reliant,' said Geoffrey. 'But I feel I have too much of my father's money behind me to be truly free.'

'Don't feel too bad,' replied Debra cheekily. 'Now we got some of your father's money behind us too!' I'd seen her like this after fights before. It was the closest to drunk she got.

'I don't think asceticism comes into it either,' I continued. 'Strive to be comfortable with your money if rich is who you are. Just don't let it take over.'

'Like it did when I was rewarding you?'

I just shrugged. I was getting a little tired of post fight philosophy.

Debra leaned playfully towards Geoffrey and said, 'I'll tell you a secret about O'Brien. He reached a state of autonomy a long time ago but, do you know what his problem is?'

'Tell me,' said Geoffrey. Interested.

'He liked it there so much, he come back to drag everyone else along with him.'

I looked at her. I tried a disapproving look, but with the way she was dressed it was difficult.

'Home time, lady. Let's get you out of those wet things.'

'Things ain't wet,' she said, pinching the top of her bustier between her thumb and forefinger then letting it twang back against her flesh, sending a pleasing wobble across her cleavage.

'Oh, they will be.'

14

It was around 10am. I was treating myself to a lie-in. Debs had been up bright and early and was at a 9am lecture, even though our postcoital bedtime had only been about four hours ago. She would easily catch up later and I'd be heading back up the M1 by the afternoon. My aching body was urging me back to sleep but sunlight was streaming through the gap in the curtains and tickling my senses. Colours were vivid. Heightened state of awareness. Sex and violence can do that to you – both could be classed as 'near death experiences' – making you more appreciative of normal life when you first step back into the flow of it but soon wearing off until the next time. Definition of a drug?

I absently watched an army of dust motes suspended in the air and illuminated in the shaft of morning sun. I thought briefly whether I should switch the TV on and swap dust for either *Kilroy* or *Trisha*. I stayed with the dust.

Then there was a knock at the door. I told

myself that, as it was not my house, I was free to ignore it. The second knock had a 'do not ignore this knock' quality to it, so I kicked off the duvet and got up. Casting my eyes round for my shirt, I realised Debra had decided she was wearing it to Uni that morning. Sporting only my black Calvin Kleins, I sucked in my gut and headed downstairs for the front door. I intercepted it just as the third knock was starting.

Standing on the doorstep was Detective Sergeant Val Townley. She was wearing a grey trouser suit, Moschino or similar, with a wide lapel lilac blouse. I sucked in my gut some more.

'How did you find me?' I asked.

'I'm a detective,' she replied deadpan.

It was a good line. I'd used it myself before now.

'How can I help you?'

'Try putting some clothes on, O'Brien. I haven't had breakfast yet and you're in danger of putting me off.'

'I'll go find a shirt. And, if you manage not to wound my pride any further, I might even be able to make you some toast.'

It was a genuine offer, but it was me also trying to check out how 'official' this visit was. She didn't respond either way, just stepped into the hall and waited for me to indicate a place to sit in the front room. I was back down in a flash. Dark blue Quicksilver short sleeve shirt on but still bare legged. Rebel, that's me.

'Coffee?' I asked. Val said milk, one sugar. Debs liked her coffee and had invested in a proper espresso maker, amongst other things, when she'd shared the reward money for finding Trevini's daughter. I made it half the strength I normally would, as I didn't want to send Val into anaphylactic shock. For toast, I could either raid Debra's food cupboard or one of the other students.'

'Unleavened Syrian barley bread or thick sliced Mighty White?' I shouted through to the front room.

'Biccys will do,' came the reply.

Ginger snaps were what I could find. Not the worst coffee biscuit in the world. I sat at right angles to Val. Her on the couch and me in an armchair. She picked up a ginger snap and examined it like it had been a long time since she'd last seen one.

'If you're suffering any morning sickness – that's yer fella,' I said, just for something to say.

'Chance would be a fine thing,' she snorted.

I presume she was referring to her busy schedule rather than lack of male attention. She looked eminently impregnatable from where I was sitting.

'So, Val, what brings you this side of the river?'

'Investigating a violent incident that occurred *my* side of the river last night.'

'Oh, really?'

'Yes, really,' she said, moistening her mouth with coffee and wiping away a crumb from her lip.

'A racially motivated violent incident?'

'Possibly. Were you by any chance involved in a violent incident yourself last night, Mr O'Brien?'

Mr now. Formal. I realised she was looking at the mouse under my right eye.

'I have a sexually predatorial girlfriend who can get a bit rough at times.'

Well, it wasn't a lie.

She seemed to ponder my sex life for a few moments, chewing more ginger snap, before replying.

'I point you in the direction of The Bucket yesterday lunchtime. Less than 24 hours later, three of their regulars are in hospital beds, two are limping and pissing blood and one of them squeaks every time he tries to talk.'

'It's a rough pub. You tried to warn me.'

'I'd like you to come with me to Bexley-heath nick. Assist us with our enquiries.'

'Am I being charged?'

'Not at present. Only one of the victims is willing to talk to us, but your name happens to have come up in the talking.'

'ID parade?'

'No. It's not what you think. Just come along, will you?' She drained her coffee, grimaced a little and stood up, smoothed her hand down the back of her trousers as if they were a skirt and looked at me expectantly.

I excused myself and went upstairs to pull on a pair of grey Dickies cords and an old pair of Vans – no socks. Grabbed my wallet and checked it for funds. The police rarely give you a lift home when they've finished with you. Did I have funds? Two rolls of bank notes winked filthily at me from on top of the bedside cabinet. I peeled off three twenties and shoved them in my wallet for the sake of it before heading back down the stairs.

'Let's go then,' I said, holding the front door open for her.

'How co-operative,' she smiled. 'I was rather hoping I'd have to arrest you.'

'Why so?'

'I just wanted to show you my handcuffs. I'll bet they're a lot nicer than your girlfriend's...'

As I was ushered through the custody area I got the feeling I was being carefully studied. I felt like I had spinach on my teeth until I realised that I was probably being stared at because the story had gone round that some guy had singlehandedly taken out six of their local hard men. I began to feel better about being studied. We've all got an ego.

Val led me into an interview room. A guy was already sat in there. He looked tired and bored and lonely. When he caught my eye though, a little light seemed to go on inside him. He suppressed it quickly but I'd seen it. He was momentarily pleased to see me. If he'd had a tail it would have wagged.

It was John. The guy with the dog from last night. The one I'd been playing pool with. The one who'd had his bollocks kicked either side of his neck by Debra.

'Jonathon Pasloe,' said Val, by way of an introduction.

She then proceeded to explain how we'd all come to be seated in this room together. She was obviously saying it for my benefit but she was presenting John with little opportunities along the way to nod in confirmation of what she was saying.

Basically, a police patrol had attended the incident in Lewisham not too long after we'd made our exit. Two ambulances had been called to mop up the mess. None of the victims had wanted to talk about what had happened. This had the effect of making the police more suspicious rather than less. Police National Computer checks linked those involved to organised racist activities and a varied list of charges and convictions. Regional Crime Squad had an interest in Malc in particular. Apparently he had an older brother called Ray who had been involved in some even heavier stuff but had dropped off all the radar screens quite a while ago. Other checks had revealed that the lads had all recently either been questioned by the Thamesmead Community Safety Unit or that there were warrants out for them.

I felt like an eejit. It sounded like the police had been pretty much on top of things in their slow yet methodical way. In a way that was likely to secure convictions. My involvement had probably blown that. Geoffrey Sitcha would find it very difficult to testify against these guys at any point in the future without impeaching himself.

Val had been up since around the time I had got to bed. She was trying to salvage something from my blundering. Hence the presence of Jonathon Pasloe. He had seemed like the weakest link so Val had been pushing away at him. He'd been bearing up pretty well until she'd managed to throw my name into the bargain to test his reaction. It had worked. He'd started spilling like a burst dam.

He'd told her everything. Well, nearly. No one seemed to be mentioning either Debs or Geoffrey. I realised that John had gone down immediately with a flaming groin, which had caused him to pass out. He never registered Geoffrey's presence at all and he probably thought that Debs was just a scared prostitute fighting back who'd given him a lucky shot.

He was convinced I'd twatted the six of them and rescued the poor girl.

And here he was, staring at me like I was Batman, Mick Foley and David Beckham rolled into one.

He said how much he hated the life he was leading and the friends he had. How he was too frightened to do anything about it. He said he knew there was something 'different' about me. Rather than this making him suspicious, he just thought of me as *better* than him and his friends. He hadn't really questioned it when I'd wanted to go along with them but it all seemed to make perfect sense when I'd turned round and attacked them. I was a hero – and he wanted to be just like me! I think it probably helped that I hadn't personally hit him either.

He was obviously still cagey when he spoke about criminal intent on his own or his friends' part – not wanting to admit too much. But Val explained that John was not being charged with anything. He'd waited at the station for a chance to meet me again. After discussion with Val he had agreed to turn police informant, but only with my blessing. Only if I thought it was the right thing for him to do.

I told John that I thought he was doing the right thing. I told him I'd be heading back up to Bradford soon but that it would be nice to go for a drink when I was down in London again. He looked happy.

Val showed me out. She looked happy too. Well, she looked amused.

From my wallet I gave her a business card in case she might want to contact me. The card said,

O'Brien's the Man. It's the word on the Street. And he gets more ass than a toilet seat.

She managed to look less amused.

I went for a wonderfully greasy breakfast before heading back to North London. Over a meal of sausage, egg, bacon, mushrooms, hash browns, fried slice, toast and tea – no beans or toms – and a cursory examination of Jordan's latest antics as reported in the *Daily Star*, I pondered over what it meant to be approved of. I liked being liked. Did it matter who did the liking? How would you feel if you knew that Hitler thought you were a good bloke? I could only conclude that, although not objectionable, it was not a comfortable feeling. It was like being fancied by a complete boiler – you feel a little insulted that they could even think they had a chance, like you're being dragged down to their level by the very act of their attention.

Debs – who is the opposite of a complete boiler – was back home by the time I returned. We enjoyed an hour or two of un-frantic massage and love-making before I hit the road. I returned to the North of England under dark skies and without fanfare. My cat would be just as pleased to see me as Jonathon Pasloe had been, but would hide it better.

I would sleep well and tomorrow I would buy new trainers and renew old friendships.

15

I didn't know what to take to Linzi Delaney. Grapes, chocolates, flowers, cigarettes, magazines? Nope. I remembered Linzi as a bright shining light who was beginning to link back into her previous social circle as soon as Rob was out of the picture. She'd have tons of visitors, to be sure. She'd be swamped with all the usual shit.

It came back to me that we had been to a particular restaurant together. There had been a glass cabinet that contained samples of the desserts that were available. She had been awe-struck by the Tower of Babel proportions of a profiterole display. She'd never seen them before. But we'd both already demolished a rich steamed pudding of shredded pigeon, rabbit and bacon which had been accompanied by shallot strewn mash, creamed lentils, and a sorrel sauce – so we were fit for nowt but sorbet by then.

Anyway, I'd offered to make profiteroles for her some other time. So I decided this was the time. I wasn't intimidated. Though I cook, baking isn't my strong point and I have more success with choux pastry than I ever do with shortcrust or flaky. It's prepared more like a sauce than a pastry and I'm fine with sauces.

As the butter slowly liquefied in the heating water I thought back over my acquaintance with Linzi Delaney. It was now about two and a half years since I'd met her. To be honest, I hadn't had a great deal to do with her since the divorce. We'd run into each other in town a couple of times and chatted away with big warm smiles on our faces, saying we must meet up again soon but never got around to it. I'd had a good luck card from her when I'd set up the PI business and we exchanged text messages as soon as we both had mobiles. One night she'd been in Zeds when I was working the door. We couldn't really chat because of the noise level and the constant stream of punters. That night I contented myself just watching her every now and then, men circling around her like feeding sharks. She dealt with any advances with an easy laugh and a toss of her beautiful hair.

She seemed a picture of fun and freedom.

I was curious as to what had now gone wrong in her life to gain her an admission to the Heights. As well as feeling guilty on my own part for not keeping in touch, I felt a little miffed that she hadn't contacted me – especially if she was in some sort of trouble. O'Brien the Rescuer.

I rescued the butter and water from the boil and dumped the flour in. Beat it until it was one lump of yellow putty. Not a gram of it stuck to the side of the pan. I got the skills to pay the bills.

I argued ineffectually with an Oxford historian on Radio 4 whilst the putty cooled. By the time I'd beaten in the eggs to a glossy finish I was conceding that she did indeed have a valid point. O'Brien the Magnanimous.

With the buns baked to golden brown and the cream whipped, I added a really personal touch. I pushed a malteser into the centre of each bun before piping in the cream and then erecting the edifice. Let the whole thing chill in the fridge whilst I was melting the Bournville. When I poured the hot, runny chocolate over the cooled profiteroles it began to harden quickly, providing a sweet superstructure, a confectionery cage.

I needed a big container to get it to Lindlea Heights. A cardboard box would have done, except that it would have detracted from the grandeur. I'd planned ahead though. Whilst out shopping for the ingredients that morning I'd bought two of the largest tins of chocolates you can get. One was Roses and the other was Quality Street. I didn't want to take sides. They were well expensive but then I wasn't short of a bob or too after my trip down to the smoke.

I emptied the tins and fashioned a large cylindrical metal container for the profiteroles by placing one upside down on top of the other. I sellotaped them in the middle but then covered that with a big pink bow from a card shop. I'd bought her a card too. The discarded choccies now filled a carrier bag to bursting.

Like I said, I thought she'd already have plenty of chocolates so I was thinking I'd drive over to Kelp's afterwards and give them to him. Then I got to thinking that he'd only be offended at such a poorly presented – if extra large – pick and mix. I'd take him out for some beers instead. I was making my way slowly through the traffic along Manningham Lane by now. With the tin, the bag and the card all beside me on the passenger seat. There were lots of dental surgeries and other private clinics in the grand old buildings to my left. A large sign on the front lawn of one place proclaimed itself as a *Weight Control Centre*. It listed such services as liposuction & liposculpture, hypnotherapy, nutritional counselling, medical advice and support (which meant prescriptions of amphetamine). It looked like it was a residential establishment too. I pulled the car over, strolled up their driveway, rang their bell, dumped six kilos of chocolate on their doorstep, and legged it.

When I got to the reception area up at the Heights, I told them the ward I was going to. The same security guard as last time wanted to know what was in the tin. I told him it was a cake. I thought I'd probably have to explain to him what profiteroles were and I didn't want the hassle. He started umming and erring about whether I could take it in with me. I was incredulous.

'We might have to search it,' he said. He sounded serious in an unsure-of-himself kind of way.

'What you gonna do? X-ray it?' Perhaps the Heights was starting to think it was Ashworth.

'Well, *examine* it, or something...'

I gave him the angriest stare I've got.

'Don't fuck with my profiteroles...' I growled. If it wasn't the toughest thing I've ever said, it had to be the campest.

'I'm sorry but we've had a bit of a drug problem here...'

'Problem? You want a problem? I suggest you open that door...'

Us cooks can get pretty damn shirty.

Tattoo-neck backed down and buzzed me in. Some security guard.

When I got up to *Ashlands* I was greeted at the desk by a blonde waif-like creature with a sallow complexion and a nose stud. She was trying hard to look totally disinterested in everything – myself included. When I said I was there to see Linzi it definitely got her attention but with a strange reaction. She sort of stared at me in blank shock for a moment then she got up and scurried into the team office. I craned my neck round to listen at the door, but all I could sense was urgency, confusion and embarrassment. I could see through the window of the door to the white-board on the wall that held a room plan with client's names on, colour coded depending on which consultant they were under. Linzi's name was nowhere to be seen. In fact, there was an empty space on the female corridor. An empty bed is rare in psychiatry. There's normally another poor soul marked on the periphery of the whiteboard ready to take the bed as soon as there's any movement. The space where her name should have been looked like it had been carefully and respectfully cleaned rather than just wiped off. It looked very final. I was starting to feel extremely uneasy. Suddenly, I didn't want to talk to any ward staff. I became acutely aware of the massive tin I was carrying. It felt awkward, stupid and incongruous. So did I.

I was already heading back out of the door as the petite blonde emerged warily from the office door and said, 'I'm sorry, but are you a relative?'

I pretended not to hear and just kept going, down the stairs and along the corridor. Mercifully or not, Asif Hasan was coming the other way up the corridor. He didn't look particularly happy but his face managed to fall even further when he saw me.

'Chris. I presume you have heard?' He was so solemn.

'What, Asif? What's happened?'

'Linzi is dead, Chris.' His words, no matter how softly spoken, sounded as harsh as a terrible insult. I swallowed hard.

'What happened? What have you done to her?' My voice grated like fingernails down a blackboard. I thought immediately of dangerous doses of intra-muscular sedatives, of lung crushing restraint positions against an unforgivingly thin carpet. I wanted to blame psychiatry for her death. It was the easy way. But I knew that those kinds of deaths were extremely rare and were accidental rather than abusive.

'It was suicide. Two nights ago. She jumped from a railway bridge. She had absconded through the fire doors after setting off the alarm. I'm sorry we lost her, Chris. But there were other patients to protect too.'

The factual coldness of his words stung me. I think they were meant to. I knew the score. If someone wanted to kill themselves then they would do it. Staff were well aware of their powerlessness in the wider scheme of things, and even if it wasn't out of any sense of compassion, a death in psychiatry shook everyone. It put everyone in their place.

'Is there somewhere you want to go and sit, Chris?'

'No Asif. Thanks. Not in this place.' I would want to speak to him at some point. My mind was still hungry for details of what

151

had happened to Linzi. Even more so than before. But I needed to go somewhere and mourn right now. I started to walk away but then turned back.

'Asif. Could you do something for me?'

'Of course, Chris. What?'

'Let me out the back way.'

Asif had a security swipe card to let me through a locked door that led out into an overflow car park between the hospital proper and the squat villas of the psychotherapy department round the back. I had suddenly felt a real need to avoid the same security guard who'd been there on the way in. I wouldn't have been able to stand any comment he might have made about my early departure or the large tin I had defended with pride. I realised now why he had been acting over-officiously. Just doing his job. He might have been on duty the night she died. He might have been out searching the grounds for Linzi whilst I was boozing and playing pool half a world away.

My legs felt weak and my head was fuzzy. I went over to a bench to sit down. I placed the tin gently beside me, careful not to break any of the chocolate strands or smudge any of the cream. As I did so, I was suddenly consumed with petty rage. Why was I being careful? What the hell did it matter now? She was gone.

I hefted the tin at the nearby wall of a pebble-dashed maintenance building. I don't know if I was expecting something more dramatic. An explosion? Or the shattering of my beautiful gift into a thousand tiny shards that would be borne away by the four winds never to be seen again?

The tin gave a muffled clang before dropping to the ground, where it rattled as it rolled back and forth slightly. It hadn't even split open.

I kicked it. Another clang as it rebounded from the wall, rolled back towards me and fell in half at my feet, where the ruined contents slopped out.

It was a fucking mess. So was I.

I went back to the bench and flopped down heavily. I took in a deep breath, fighting tears, before holding my head in my hands and gazing dejectedly down at the floor.

It was then that I saw it. Stuck to the front of my Doc Marten, amidst splatters of cream, was a single malteser.

I picked it, very carefully, off my shoe and just stared at it long enough for any passing psychiatrist to declare me insane.

'Thanks Linzi,' I managed to say quietly just as my throat constricted and my sobbing took over, 'I shall treasure this.'

16

I drove without really thinking to the end of Chellow Dean and spent a couple of hours walking the length of the woods to and fro. Linzi and I had walked there. I skimmed some stones, or attempted to, across the surface of the reservoir. We'd done that together too.

The sky was now white, heavy and electric. This spring afternoon felt like a summer evening. I'd welcome a storm, but it would be hours yet. Might not even happen at all.

Back in the car, none of the music on the radio or my tapes seemed appropriate. I rolled slowly and silently over a long downward slope of speed bumps through Girlington, avoiding grubby children who played without any hint of either joy or road sense. I pulled up onto the pavement across the road from a dilapidated but busy general store. All metal shutters and boxes of stringy, smelly veg outside. I had a plan to buy some booze and fags and just wallow in it. I would listen to a tape of Eva Cassidy when I got home and I would probably hug the cat too hard and make it run off. Yep, me and my self-pity would make a night of it together.

Coming out of the shop with twenty Silk Cut and a bottle of less-than-full-strength blended whisky, I couldn't help but notice four Asian youths gathered around the front of my Escort. One of them, in fact, slouching on the bonnet, one foot on the road and one on my bumper. When Slouch saw I was heading towards the car he called to me, 'You shouldn't have parked here, innit? Dis where we park, Brudda.'

I don't mean he said 'brother' with an accent. He actually *meant* to sound like that. There was, indeed, a shitty Subaru with penis-extension exhaust pipe and other laughable accessories, pulled uncomfortably close up to my rear end.

I had to walk past them to get to the driver's side. Without breaking my stride, I strolled close by as if I hadn't heard a thing and right hooked him on the cheek with the arm that wasn't holding the whisky. It wasn't enough to break anything but it knocked him on his ass. I was at my driver door now. I switched my shopping to my right hand, fumbled for my key with the left, and got in the car whilst they all stood frozen in disbelief. I fired up the engine, powered down the electric window, and said,

'It's all right. I'm leaving now. You might want to get your mate out of the way of my fucking car though...' And I revved the engine.

They sprang into action by dragging the poor lad hurriedly onto the pavement. As I drove off, I could see in the rear view that he was now on his feet and appeared to be starting on one of his mates who'd just helped him up.

The normal me would have struck up a conversation, just to show how unintimidated I was. The normal me might even have made four new friends.

I guess I was having a bad day. The poor lad had just been in the wrong place at the wrong time and had mouthed off to the wrong person.

When I got back there was an ansaphone message from Debs, asking how I was. Debs won't ask unless she's prepared to hear a proper answer so I thought I would call her back. I'd never mentioned Linzi to her. It had never cropped up during the time we'd been together and I'd kind of put things to one side with the Geoffrey Sitcha thing. All I'd mentioned to Debs was that I was going to visit an old friend in hospital when I got back.

So I phoned her and poured it all out. She was wonderful. You just know with Debs that she'll either be supportive or recognise her limitations and say so. She won't do anything to make you feel worse. She won't add her own insecurities into the bargain. Debra doesn't do insecure. There was no 'Why haven't you told me about her before?' or 'Did you love her more than you love me?' She just plain listened.

When I'd finished talking she could hear my tears in the silence.

She said, 'I'll read you something,' and I listened to her light footfalls as she paced across to her well-stocked bookcase. I could hear her sink back down on the sofa and the rustling of pages before she spoke again.

'When I am dead, my dearest,
Sing no sad songs for me;
Plant thou no roses at my head,
Nor shady cypress tree:
Be the green grass above me

157

With showers and dewdrops wet;
And if thou wilt, remember,
And if thou wilt, forget.'

Debra paused for breath. Before she continued, I swear I felt warm breath on my shoulder. From across the miles, or further beyond? Distant thunder rumbled. The storm had broken.

'I shall not see the shadows,
I shall not feel the rain;
I shall not hear the nightingale
Sing on, as if in pain:
And dreaming through the twilight
That doth not rise nor set,
Haply I may remember,
And haply may forget.'

I was silent for a while before responding. 'That was beautiful. Who was it?'
'It was a woman telling you to grieve without hurting. Whether it was Linzi Delaney, or Debra Prentice, or Christina Rossetti, don't matter. Just take it to your heart, OB.'
'I will. Do you know what, Debra?'
'What?'
'I love you.'
'I know you do.'

We both paused. We both knew what I was going to say.

'I'm going to find out what happened to Linzi Delaney.'

'I know you are,' came the answer that I knew was coming.

I remembered her mum saying the same thing to me last autumn when I promised to find the people who hurt her son. It was said with the same compassion for my own feelings, and the same confidence and trust in my word, that I wasn't sure I had myself.

I watched a bit of telly before going to bed. The cat made a point of sitting on top of the set and draping its tail across the middle of the screen. I didn't go over and right hook it. I admitted to myself for the first time that I had loved Linzi Delaney. It felt odd to be that honest with myself. I held onto the feeling for a while then let it go. As soon as I did, a wave of love for Debra washed over me. I smiled to myself. I felt a bit more like the normal me.

I drank the whisky, but I didn't touch the cigarettes.

17

I hadn't got round to buying the New Balance running shoes yesterday so I made do with an old pair of Hi-Tecs that weren't exactly falling apart and which only got used in moments of desperation. My other back-up trainers were Asics and lived at Debra's. She's got three pairs of Saucony – performance, trail, and extra cushioned for city running.

I inflicted an early morning run upon myself. Crunching rhythmically along the dirt road that winds steeply up Shipley Glen, following Loadpit Beck all the way up to Gilstead Moor. I stopped once when I disturbed two jays, watched their tail feathers descend brightly into the wooded valley, squinted at the rising sun glinting off the flowing beck below me, listening to the bubbling and crackling of its burgeoning waters. The woods were not yet green except for the conifers, but the silver birch were sprouting buds, the gorse bushes were rich with yellow flowers, and a lone cherry tree was in full and early blossom. Wet bark and millstone grit outcrops shone and sparkled with the remnants of last night's rain. I pretended to marvel at nature, but really it was just an excuse to rest. My body felt dry and heavy from the whisky as I pushed myself on.

When I got as high up as I'd wanted to go, I regretted that I hadn't made the run a ride. What I wouldn't give to be burning back down the way I came up on my Cannondale with the wind in my face and the bounce of the front suspension fork rattling at my wrists. I ran back down past Bracken Hall. By then I was okay, feeling loose and alive. I returned home, showered, and drove down to my office, ready for a mental workout.

On the way up I got myself a bacon, egg and mushroom teacake from the downstairs sandwich shop, fired up my coffee filter and checked the inevitable phone messages and bills before settling myself in behind my desk. I booted up the PC and made a list of people I might want to speak to about Linzi. It started with those whose contact had been most recent – hospital staff. Asif would be a key person, and there were a few other people up there who were still on speaking terms with me. Professionalism and confidentiality would be an issue but if anyone had the means of obtaining information from up there, it was me.

Her parents were on the list. A meek and mild old couple who had lost contact with her during her time with Rob Delaney. I hadn't met them, but they had sent me a card once they had been reunited with her – thanking me for my help and saying that she spoke highly of me. Much of her adolescence they had been antagonistic because of her relationship with Rob but she had since become much closer to them after the divorce. I would have to visit them. Mr and Mrs Trueman if I remembered correctly.

That's when it struck me, what Asif Hasan had said that day – 'Linzi *Morgan*. Her married name was Delaney.' I'd hardly registered it as odd. Just the experience of seeing her there that day was odd enough.

So she hadn't gone back to her maiden name. I had remembered her saying that she wouldn't, that she would only change her name if she remarried. She felt the name Delaney gave her a little power around the streets and bars of Bradford. I guess that was okay, it was about the only good thing Rob ever gave her. I remember her saying, with a twinkle in her eye, that she wouldn't mind another Irish surname. I remember my heart beating faster.

So had she got remarried? If she had, I would be speaking to her husband too. But then why had Asif put it that way. 'Her married name was Delaney.' Why hadn't he referred to it as her first marriage?

Questions.

I got on with my list. There was one of her girlfriends' names I remembered. Then I added Rob and some other members of the Delaney family to the list. Well, I had to get to them eventually.

I went online to do some background checks on the people I had. Addresses, current professions, anything I could get. What I didn't expect was an article from the *Telegraph* about a fatal car accident at the back end of January, on treacherous black ice between Thornton Road and Queensbury. Occupants of the vehicle – a Mr and Mrs Trueman and their daughter, a Miss Delaney. Fortunately, Miss, Delaney had been miraculously thrown clear through the back window. Unfortunately for Miss Delaney, it appeared that she had lain helplessly broken-limbed but still conscious as she watched her parents burn to death in the wreckage.

Maybe that would have been enough to satisfy my curiosity. A hospital admission for her injuries. A transfer to psychiatric care when her grief became too difficult for the 'normal nurses' to bear. The nightmare of an acute ward, the worse nightmare of having no normality to go back to if you left. Two months of being locked in the Catch 22 of wanting life to be different to how it is. Enough to drive her to her death.

But why hadn't I heard from her during that time? And why the change of surname whilst she was in hospital?

I checked around for an article about her suicide. It only merited a couple of lines the evening after its occurrence. No mention of a name. I'm sure some bright spark of a journo would be looking into it right now and would at least link it back to the car accident.

I couldn't be bothered with the rest of the list now. Something had gone on up at the Heights and the best place to find out about it all was the hospital itself. I phoned first to at least check if Asif was going to be around, he might be down at the infirmary assessing overdoses. I didn't fancy a protracted con-versation with any of the reception staff so I assumed the persona of a doctor and threw in a few bits of lingo that would open the channels of communication.

'Hello? It's Dr. Robert here. I'm SHO over at the PICU in York. I'd like to speak to Dr. Hasan about a recent ECR from yourselves. I've got a bloody tribunal in the works and he acted in Section 12 approved capacity for the original detention, so I want to pick his brains.'

They got me to hold the line whilst they bleeped him and patched it through to the nearest available phone. The receptionist must have garbled some of my jargon to him before putting me through. He sounded confused but happy to help.

'Excuse me for my ignorance, Dr...'

'Dr Robert. It's a Beatles song.'

'O'Brien?'

'I toyed with using Dr. Andthemedics, but I couldn't pull off the Greek accent...'

'You know I am not supposed to talk to you?'

'What?'

'I presumed that's why you used the subterfuge...

'No. That was just me pratting about. What's going on?'

'An investigation. Possibly an inquest.

Staff have been instructed that they will not speak to journalists or anyone unofficial who is asking questions. You, personally, will be turned away at reception if you arrive.'

'Well, we need to talk.'

'As I have said, I cannot speak to you on pain of disciplinary action. If you attempt to accost me whilst I am eating my meal at 7pm this evening at the Paan house, then I shall have no choice but to get up and leave.'

'Thanks, Asif,' I said. I replaced the receiver and stared at it for a time, whilst I considered what dishes I might fancy tonight.

With a few hours to kill, no one else to talk to, and the prospect of a large calorific intake looming, I hit the gym.

I avoided the free weights and just did some light pumping on the machines. I'd given up trying to put on more muscle quite a while back. Now I just want to keep what I've got and make it more tightly packed. Besides, I was still aching from the punch-up three nights ago. As I'd done quite a run only that morning, I laid off the cardio machines. I went downstairs to the martial arts studio, which was deserted at the time, and did ten minutes with the skipping rope, a bit of stretching, then did the *Sil Lim Tao*

and the *Bil Jee* forms from Wing Chun –
twice each, fast and slow.

When I'd done, I took a long hard look at
myself in the large dusty mirror that ran the
length of the wall. My muscles were pleas-
ingly pumped and gleaming with sweat. My
midriff was a little softer than I'd have liked it
to be. My left pectoral, right biceps and right
eye were all bruised. Dark bruises that would
become even darker before they faded.

I could hear my own breath unnaturally
loud in the silence.

I didn't like my short hair.

I paused briefly on my way out of the door
to turn and bow to the empty room. This
sacred space, on a daily basis, played host to
better men than I.

A shit, a shave and shower. Booted and
suited, off to the *Murghaz*. Well, not exactly
suited. Black Base loafers, black Burberry
Jeans and a grey Jonathon Adams short
sleeve shirt with black dragon motif.

If the *Murghaz* were cheaper, it would be
the best all round curry house in Bradford.
It's a good place to go if you want to impress
a dining partner. Weekday evening and there
was even a small queue to get in. Asif already
had a table for two though and waved me
through. We shook hands as I sat.

'Busy,' he said.

'I had to park a way off, up Great Horton road.'

We both had the *Machalay Rosti*. Whole fish baked in a heaven of spices. It was new to the menu. We agreed between mouthfuls that this might account for the place being so packed.

I started with the questions. It had to happen sooner or later.

'*Me personally?*' I asked.

'We are not allowed to talk with anyone about it, but your name has been mentioned as someone who might try to ask questions.'

'Well, asking questions is pretty much my job description. Who mentioned me? Was I named in an inter-office memo or something?'

'No. This has all been passed round verbally.' He paused and swallowed, although he had not taken a morsel of food for some moments now.

'It's not pleasant, Chris,' he added.

'I can't imagine that it is,' I replied.

'Linzi was admitted in a state of Post Traumatic Stress. She subsequently underwent Psychotherapy...'

'You mean Bereavement Counselling, Asif? Her parents had just died. In front of her. I hardly think anyone's gonna go digging for underlying causes for her distress...'

'Nevertheless. Her Psychotherapist felt there was evidence of past abuse...'

I was gritting my teeth and clutching the edges of the table now. Livid.

'...and now there are people saying that *you* were involved in the abuse.'

I was speechless. Gift of the gob was speechless.

'I'm sorry, Chris.'

It took me a little while before I could whisper, 'Not as sorry as some lying fucker's gonna be.'

18

'Do you want me to order you another beer?' Asif asked kindly.

'Better make it two.'

He started to remind me that he didn't drink, but then twigged. A short burst of Urdu to one of the waiters and a couple of fresh bottles of Kingfisher were placed in front of me. Drops of condensation speckled the surface of the pale green glass. I felt like placing one to my hot, angry face and holding it there until I had cooled.

I took almost half of the first bottle in one pull. There was nothing wrong with it, but it couldn't take away the bitter taste I had in my mouth.

'Right. You know I'm not an abuser, or you wouldn't be talking to me. Right? So let's just leave all the bullshit to one side for a moment. Who is Linzi Morgan? I knew her as Delaney. She was still Delaney at the time of the accident. Her maiden name was Trueman.'

Asif sighed. He suddenly looked very old. He shook his head slowly before speaking.

'She was one of *Morgan's Babies*.'

'What?'

'You will remember Jodie Morgan?'

I repeated the name back to him incredulously. I had known Jodie Morgan. When I had worked for Bradford Health, she was a jumped-up Hitler with some sort of half-arsed management diploma. She had no qualification in medicine, nursing, or any other sort of therapy. That had never stopped her from interfering though. What did she have to do with this?

'Jodie Morgan is now head of psychology department. Clinical Director,' Asif told me.

'How did that happen? She's not qualified.'

'She went on a course of study. The Trust paid for it. She returned from her course straight into the post. None of the clinicians were happy about it.'

'But no one challenged it?'

'Those who spoke out most vociferously are no longer with the Trust.'

'Jesus.'

I shouldn't have been surprised. I knew how it worked. But I just couldn't imagine Jodie Morgan being let loose on clients. She was bad enough with staff, and they were supposed to have the defences to deal with it.

'What the bejaysus is a *Morgan's baby?*'

'It's what we all called the women who were involved in her Survivors of Abuse therapy. It was meant as an in-joke, a criticism even, but when Morgan heard, she took it as a compliment.'

'What's that got to do with Linzi changing her surname?'

'It was a prerequisite of getting into therapy.'

'*What?*'

I was using that word a lot.

'To demonstrate commitment to the therapeutic process. Something about the rejection of patriarchy too. She encouraged her patients to see themselves as part of her *therapy family*.'

I didn't say 'What?' again. I sat there and rocked in my seat with unspeakable fury, involuntarily pecking my head forwards in little bursts, like a chicken. I eventually spat out a reply.

'Now *that* ... is ... fucking ... abuse.'

Asif nodded. He looked guilty. He told me that he was sorry. He had been keeping his head down and doing his medical bit – letting the suits and the cardigans worry about their bit whilst he did his. Talking about it now, naming the Devil, made it clear that some unacceptable things were going on in the Trust. I told him to quit being part of the problem and be part of the solution. He asked what the solution was. I said it was me. He didn't look one hundred percent convinced, but he kept answering my questions.

'How long has this been going on?' I asked.

'It would be about eight months now.'

'Is anyone monitoring the clinical effectiveness of her "therapy family"?'

'Not formally, as far as I am aware. From what I know, she has two women who now attend her sessions as outpatients. One could possibly presume they are happy with the process. I believe there are another two who are currently in-patients. Long-term in-patients. They may be going through the motions in order to effect a discharge. I know of one former attendee who has been transferred to a secure unit following an incident of fire setting. And, of course, there has been one suicide.'

I sat and thought for a while. Drank some more beer.

'I don't like it,' I said finally, almost to myself.

'You do not surprise me, Chris.'

'The whole thing is dodgy,' I expanded. 'Linzi must have had a rough time of it, but I know her – *knew* her. She'll have been looking for someone to help her; she'll have been open to it. She didn't want to die. I know it.'

'Not everyone wants to be rescued, Chris. Especially from such great pain.'

'Someone should have helped her,' I continued. 'No one did. It looks to me like the opposite happened. Hippocratic Oath, Asif, *Keep from Harm and Injustice*. Someone screwed up.'

'You feel guilt that you were not available to her?'

'Oh get fucked, will ya!' I barked, slamming a now empty bottle down on the table and rocking my chair back slightly.

He'd gone quiet. Asif and I do banter and he's certainly used to me swearing, but I think it was the first time I'd ever sworn *at* him. I quickly made amends, but continued my diatribe.

'Linzi was in a bad situation that was made actively worse. I want to point the finger. I want to investigate. I want to know if it was sheer incompetence or wilful abuse. Then I want to look the perpetrator in the eye and say "you're shit" or "you're evil" respectively.'

'I can't see an inquest putting it as bluntly as that...'

'That's why it needs me to do it.'

'May I ask who or what you are doing it *for?*'

'Dangerous ground again, Asif. Does it really matter?'

'I am only trying to focus your anger.'

I drew breath. I was angry. I should deal with it. Crime to spoil a good meal.

'I'd like to say I'm doing it for Linzi, but that's pretty lame. I could say that I'm doing it for anyone like her – who might otherwise end up on the receiving end of a therapist's personal agenda. I could say I'm trying to clear my name – except that, thinking about it, I couldn't give a rat's ass what the mud-slingers up there think of me. Really, I'm just going to do it because it's what I do.'

'Are you like the moth to the flame?'

I thought about that for a while, and then replied.

'No. I choose this. I could walk away if I wanted to and part of me would love to avoid the hassle.' I thought for a moment before asking Asif a question in return, 'Why do you do the work you do?'

'I'm sure you have heard the phrase – "it pays the rent".'

'But there are many ways of doing that. Why did you become a psychiatrist, Asif?'

He blinked a few times, and then looked around the room as if someone else might offer an answer. Finally, he gave a little shrug and spread his hands.

'Apart from parental encouragement to become a "proper" doctor – I had a natural interest, which I pursued, found that I was capable of the work, and here I am.'

'There you go. Magic word. *Capable*. I do this because I *can*. I always thought it was going to be somebody else's job to right the wrongs, but I discovered I could do it too.'

'No one will be paying your rent for this particular investigation, will they?'

'I'll live.'

'What are you going to do, Chris?'

That question always used to throw me, but I was getting a bit more practised at this.

'Talk to some people. Get some background. Find out as much as I can about Jodie Morgan. Find out why the finger is being pointed at me.'

'You might upset some people along the way.'

'I'll live.'

19

The next morning I went to see my friend, Susie. Her place was not far from the Heights. A large old cottage off the top of Smith Lane. The stonework was dark millstone grit, blackened by Bradford's industrial past but swathed green with ivy in nature's relentless embrace.

The sturdy timber of the front door was a vibrant mixture of red and green. I think she'd painted it that way one Christmas and hadn't got round to doing anything else with it. Part of her front window was stained glass which she had also done herself, in more subdued colours than the door. There was an area deliberately but gently clear of ivy around the doorway, where tendrils of clematis were weaving in and out of an olive wood trellis, and just starting to bud.

I paused and took it all in before knocking. This house always made me smile.

My knocking had built to a crescendo by the time she came to answer. She must have been working out the back.

'Hey Boy!' she exclaimed, putting her arms out for a hug.

I always felt like I was going to break her in two when we started to hug, yet always finished the hug remembering how wrong I was. She felt skinny and bony but soft and alive. Quiet and calm, but capable of sheer intensity. She reminded me of a cheetah.

'Get a beer from the fridge and come see what I'm working on,' she suggested, turning down the hall and leading the way.

I dutifully pulled a stubby brown bottle of watery Belgian out of the fridge. It was better than nothing. I noticed that the only other stuff in the fridge was cheese, ketchup and margarine. You'd think a vegetarian would be better organised.

I followed through to the high-walled back yard and instantly broke into a massive grin – as much at the look of pride on Susie's face as at the object of her attentions.

'It's my new camper van,' she said animatedly.

'It's certainly camper than your old van,' I agreed.

It was one of those cylindrical VW vans. In a delicate, yet still 'in yer face', shade of pink.

'What do you think?'

'I think Scooby Doo and Lady Penelope had a head on – and this is what was left of the wreckage.'

'Cheeky whippersnapper,' she replied. 'It's going to be called *The Flying Monkey*,' she explained as she pointed to the side of the vehicle.

I could see now that she had traced an outline of one of those bizarre blue creatures from *The Wizard of Oz* and was beginning to paint it with great skill and attention to detail. I could see now other outlines of characters from the film.

'Speechless, eh? I suppose you can't help being a philistine,' she chided.

'If I only had a brain...' I spread my hands

and tried looking meek.

That made her laugh. I told her that her camper van was going to be a thing of great beauty. She led me back into the house, got herself a peppermint tea, and then we sat down and got to business.

'You said on the phone that there was something going on up at the hospital. Something that involved Jodie Morgan. What's up, OB?'

'I want to pick your brains.'

'You want me to tell you about Jodie Morgan?'

'Not really...'

'You think because she's a dyke, I'm going to know all about her?'

'No...'

'Well first off, I can tell you she's not really a dyke.'

'Honestly, Suse – it wasn't quite what I was asking about, but now you've got me interested. It was kind of common knowledge up at the hospital that she played for the other team.'

'The winning team. Well, everyone up at the hospital has got it wrong then, haven't they?'

'Do tell.'

'It's what she wants people to think. Kind

of a political statement. She's only on the scene because she thinks she needs to be. She doesn't even think it's cool or anything. You can tell. She doesn't actually fancy anybody.'

'Celibate? Asexual?'

'I don't think so. The impression is that she gets up to all sorts, but it's all about power – nothing to do with loving or sharing. She's networking, making contacts. She's probably into the darker stuff – and there are people around who can connect her to some very dark stuff, if that's what she wants.'

'I think you've nailed her, Suse. Did you know she was a therapist now?'

'Good god, no!'

Which had pretty much been my reaction, as you know. The reason I had come to see Susie was nothing to do with her sexual orientation. I swear. Susie was herself a therapist. She incorporated artwork and bodywork, and sometimes even a little tarot, into her therapy but she was still more 'professional' in her approach than most of the cardigans I'd met. We'd known each other a good few years now.

I told her everything I knew about Morgan's Babies. She agreed that it was an absolutely hideous way to approach the treatment of vulnerable people. But when I told her I was thinking about tracking down some of the 'babies' and talking to them, she didn't agree.

'These are vulnerable people, OB. Likely to be even more vulnerable now that they are part of this "therapy". You'll be just another intruder on their distress – manipulating them for your own agenda.'

'It's what I do, Suse. I'm allowed to not have the same sensibilities as a therapist in my line of work.'

'If it was anyone else but you, I'd accept that argument. But you'll go in there expecting them to feel better for talking to you. Won't you?'

'Won't they? I'll be helping them.'

'You'll be trying to save them. This therapy, no matter how misguided and shite it is, is not a burning building that you can heroically drag these women out of. They can still choose to say no, even if the consequences are threatening. It is not ultimately helpful for you to do that for them.'

'Linzi's way of saying no was to kill herself.'

'True. How does that make you feel?'

'Very, very sad.'

She did a little movement with her head. The movement invited me to say more, without pressurising me to do so in any way. Surprised at myself, I carried on speaking.

'And proud. I am proud of her.'

'She resisted, and she did it by herself,' confirmed Susie.

'She couldn't have done that with Rob, she needed my help,' I added.

'She did it this time alone, although her strength cost her her life.'

'Sad. But not wrong. Not even weak. I can see that now. But there's still something wrong with the way she was treated.'

'Certainly, and I expect you to do something about it,' she smiled.

'I will. Any suggestions?'

'Go straight for the dragon, OB. Leave the fair maidens to fend for themselves.'

'Or send 'em to you?'

'That entirely depends on how fair they are, doesn't it?' She did a comedy wink.

'And you a professional! I never heard that.'

'I never said it.'

I left Susie's feeling a little clearer. I was well aware of my tendency to want to rescue people and, although it was more appropriate in my current profession than it had ever been in nursing, it still got me sidetracked and blind-sided at times. But I accept that it's part of my hardwired personality, and it hasn't got me killed yet.

Despite being warned off talking to the people who might help me to understand what was going on, it was like Suse had given me permission to go after Morgan. I was happy with that.

A spot of early lunch, a favour to call in, and I was all set for an afternoon of surveillance.

I parked across the road from the Heights, not the front entrance but the side with a direct eye line over to the psychotherapy department. First though, I got out of the car and walked towards the main entrance. As I neared the reception, a security guard began walking out towards me. I didn't stop to argue or fight. I turned and walked away, seeing behind my shoulder that he had stopped in his tracks as soon as I did so. Just checking. Then I headed back to the car and parked my arse.

I spent about forty-five minutes listening to a tape of Chris Morris's mental radio show *Blue Jam*. I had the volume right up too, with my windows down. Followed that up with some White Stripes – *De Stijl*, best thing I'd heard in years. I was wearing a black Stone Cold Steve Austin T-shirt with 'What?' emblazoned on it and a pair of Police shades. You might say I was conspicuous.

An obvious in-patient came over to me and started to tell me about the tapes that the Home Office made of his thoughts, and how he had developed an elaborate code to thwart them. I listened without prejudice. He went away when he realised I had no cigarettes to offer him.

After about another half an hour a security guard approached and said, 'Excuse me sir, but you've been parked in this spot for nearly two hours. Can I ask what you are doing here?'

'I'm busy looking good,' I replied without looking at him.

You could tell that he wished he hadn't opened the conversation with a question. He opted for a more authoritarian approach.

'Move your car.'

I decided that his rudeness was uncalled for, so came back with some of my own.

'Arrange the following words into a well known phrase or saying: Off. Fuck.'

'Have it your way,' he said petulantly, 'I'm calling the police.'

As he walked away I started screaming as

if in terror. He jumped then turned around and gazed daggers at me as I smiled back at him. I flipped him the middle finger, then he headed off back round the hospital building. Twenty minutes later, a squad car pulled in behind me.

The officer who approached me was young, broad shouldered, bespectacled and had very little hair for his age. He seemed to walk with a swagger, but that could have been all the kit he was carrying around his waist.

'You've been asked by the staff of the hospital to move your car, sir.

'Am I causing an obstruction, officer?'

'The person I spoke to feels that you are an intimidating presence to their patients.'

'Really?'

'May I see your driver's license and registration details, sir?'

I had them ready.

'O'Brien,' he said to himself before looking back at me, 'that name sounds familiar. Do you have a criminal record, Mr O'Brien?'

'Well, I've got *Journey to the Centre of the Earth* by Rick Wakeman...'

'Move your car,' he sighed, managing to sound tired yet forceful both at once.

That time I did.

I didn't move it too far though. A couple of streets away was my back-up car for the occasion. A bottle green Peugeot 206 with tinted windows, a staff car from one of the Trevini owned small businesses in Bradford that I'd been allowed to borrow for the day. I took off my shades, put a white shirt on over my t-shirt, and drove back up to the Heights. I parked on the other side of the road, facing the other way, and just sat there quietly this time.

It was like what I'd done with the phones down in London. When people think they've got one over on you, that's when they relax. That's when they're going to be particularly blind to whatever you might do next.

Jodie Morgan left the psychotherapy department at ten past four. She was wearing black leather boots with quite a heel on them, a black pencil skirt, and a chocolate brown jacket of expensive cut hanging loosely enough to reveal a white silk blouse. Being a professional observer, I could even tell that she was not wearing a bra beneath it. Her dark hair was straight but looked expensively maintained. It was quite an ensemble. She had certainly got into power dressing since I had worked for the Trust. Her face, however, still resembled

186

a bulldog licking piss off a nettle.

She walked over to a brown Mercedes-Benz SLK230 and got in. The car said 'Power' too. And it matched her jacket.

I tailed her as expertly as a white boy from the suburbs knows how. The Bradford traffic was still swollen with parents and schoolchildren but was easing off. Come five o'clock, there'd be a more potent injection as people started to leave work. Thankfully though, she didn't head for the centre, and neither did she make full use of her respectably sized engine. We went along Duckworth and Toller Lane, crawled down Carlisle Road, across the valley up to Five Lane Ends, and ended up on a little residential street between Idle and Apperley Bridge with modern but expensive houses.

She turned up a short and steep driveway, rolling the Merc slowly into a gaping garage whose door had opened automatically as she'd driven up to it. The door to the garage closed behind her. She didn't come back out. I presumed, therefore, that there was a side door from the garage into the house.

I sat and watched the house but not for long. Being the type of street that it was, someone was bound to get suspicious. What I did do was use my binoculars to read the make and model of the brightly coloured alarm system halfway up the wall above the front door. I also clocked the make of the electronic door system on the garage. Just as I was about to leave though, Jodie emerged from the front door in the company of another woman. She was a little taller than Jodie and had close cropped brown hair on a head and face that would have suited long, flowing and blonde. They were both in naff but pricey pastel shade tracksuits and nondescript trainers. They set off slowly down the street, picking up more of a jogging pace by the time they turned the corner at the bottom.

I decided I'd stay a little longer. See how long they ran for.

Twenty minutes. Both of them were sweating lightly upon their return, Jodie noticeably short of breath but not her partner. I'd learnt a couple of things. One – breaking into the house whilst they were both out on a run would probably not give me enough time for a decent snoop. Maybe if I'd known exactly what I was looking for, but not for purposes of general nosiness. And two – if I ever had to physically chase Jodie Morgan, I was pretty confident I could run her into the ground.

It was clear that a spot of house breaking was now going to be in order. I would need to commence some meticulous preparation.

The first stage of preparation involved driving home a little too fast, whilst humming the theme from *Mission Impossible* to myself.

Men.

20

It was still only just shy of half five when I got in. I decided to phone my technical support guy. It was cheeky of me, but I thought that if I could catch him before he shut up shop tonight I might save a whole morning of faffing about tomorrow.

After a couple of rings it clicked straight on to the ansaphone.

'You have reached the offices of Spies R Us. There is no one to answer your call at present. Do not take that as a green light to come and burgle us. Our security system will totally mess with you. If you wish, you can leave your name, number and query after the tone...'

'Strange? If you're there, pick up. It's OB...'

I heard the receiver being picked up and my voice ceased to echo back at me.

'O'Brien! I was just shutting up shop for the evening. To what do I owe the pleasure?'

'Any plans for this evening, Strange? Thought you might fancy a beer?'

'You're asking me out? Either you're not getting enough sexual intercourse or you need something from me.'

'Hmm. Let's just say I'd like to get my hands on your equipment.'

I could feel him blushing over the phone. For all his intellect and weirdness, Strange is essentially very shy. I guess you could call him a nerd.

But he was *my* nerd.

I broke the silence for him.

'I might bring the boy Kelp with me if that's okay. He doesn't get over to Leeds enough. We could eat at *Chung's*.'

And thus it was arranged.

As you might have gathered, Strange runs a shop in Leeds called Spies R Us. His real name is Graham. Graham Bedfellowes. He gets called Strange. Basically, the shop sells really cool gadgets. Most have some direct surveillance application but he sells lots of other little things like laser pointers and motorised scooters. I get all my stuff from Strange, right down to my fake ID cards. Some of the more expensive stuff he just lets me rent. Or borrow even. He loves it – playing Q to my James Bond.

Kelp was no problem to locate and rope in. By ten to eight I had fed the cat, taken a quick bath, put on a clean shirt and was sat between the two of them on a jade green couch with marble arm rests, each with our bottles of *Tsingtao*, waiting for a table.

'Don't they do no "all you can eat" here, man?' enquired Kelp.

'No.'

'They should.'

'How alien that would be to the *daoist* concept of moderation in all things.'

'Ahh, but when one becomes empty, surely one must then become full?' chimed Strange.

'Smart arse college kid.'

'I know you are. Doesn't make you a bad person though.'

He was getting cocky for a nerd.

'Anyway man, when was the last time you was mod-er-rate at the dining table? You about as moderate as Idi Amin,' challenged Kelp.

I ignored them for a moment, pretending

to look at the menu, then a took a breath and said, 'Duck.' Just as they started to nod in approval, I slapped them both across the back of their heads simultaneously.

'Warned you...' I shouted back at them, already on my way to the gents.

We generally dicked about for the rest of the evening. I was certainly having a better time than my last meal out. I prefer Chinese to Indian as well. We didn't start talking shop until Strange had taken us back to his premises. He and I sat through the back, whilst Kelp acted out the proverbial kid locked in a toyshop. I suppose he was. A very old kid with very expensive toys.

'Yep. This'll open the kind of garage door you're talking about. No question.'

He handed me a little box that was like a TV remote, but smaller and with less buttons.

'What about the alarm system? Have you got some sort of "code breaker" or something?'

'Code breaker?'

'You know, something I can clamp onto the control panel that will quickly run through a combination of digits until it matches the alarm and disables it.'

'Like in the movies?'

'Yeah!'

'No such thing.'

'Ahh, you're spoiling it...'

'Not for a bog standard household alarm system, anyway.'

'So, what can I do?'

'Are you bothered about whether anyone knows you've been in?'

'Couldn't care less. I just don't want to attract attention to myself whilst I'm in there, lest I don't get enough time to see what I want to see.'

'Unplug it.'

'Eh?'

'You're gaining access through the garage. Once you're in, just get to the front door – it's invariably where you'll find the control panel – and unplug it. The system you mentioned to me plugs directly into the mains and isn't linked to any call centres or the police.'

'But I'll be setting it off?'

'Only for a few seconds. No one will get suspicious if it turns straight off again. Happens all the time.'

Just then I was distracted by something trundling towards me across the smooth vinyl floor. It looked like a toaster. Or rather, it looked like a toaster would have looked like if it were playing a villain in *Mad Max 2*. Kelp appeared in the door behind it – remote control in his hand and big grin on his face.

'What the bejaysus is that?' I wanted to know as I quickly moved my foot from its path. It swung away in quite a tight arc for its dimensions and sped off across the room.

'It's Norman,' revealed Strange proudly.

Norman had spun again and was now coming back towards me. Two lethal-looking flick knives, positioned one above the other on one side of its 'body' sprung into action and pointed straight at me as Kelp pressed a button on the remote. Another press and a loud noise issued forth from somewhere within those chrome innards. 'Eeeee! Eeeee! Eeeee!' – it was the musical refrain from the shower scene in *Psycho*.

'Explain,' I demanded, placing my foot firmly on top of Norman before he could come any closer. Hoping that the soles of my Timberlands would repel any nasty surprises that might pop upwards, from what were quite definitely slots designed to hold toast.

'You're standing on the surefire winner of the next series of *Robot Wars*,' said Strange.

'Cool!' exclaimed Kelp, without any hint

of irony.

'You two,' I told them 'are deeply sad and beyond any form of psychiatric help or spiritual redemption.'

And, with that, I lifted my foot and punted Norman across the floor and through the door from whence he came.

21

I awoke realising it was the weekend. It had caught me by surprise. Once that would have been a good feeling, but now I just wanted to get on with my work. I drove past Morgan's place a couple of times on Saturday morning, saw signs of activity. Better to wait until she was going to work.

I spent the rest of the weekend arseing about on the internet, watching the wrestling and morally justifying myself to myself. Monday I would start for real.

I waited at the end of Jodie Morgan's street on Monday morning and watched her leave, presumably for work.

I still had the Peugeot for a couple of days, which was going to help with surveillance as

I could alternate between that and the Escort. They both had tinted windows and swapping them round should allow me a little longer before the locals became suspicious.

I rolled the car slowly down the length of the street, scoping the front window as I went past. Now I had to see about her partner. I'd thought about knocking on the door with some pretext to get her out of the house – tell her she'd won a vacuum cleaner but she had to be at the head office by midday to pick it up, that sort of thing. But people are falling for that one less and less these days, and I reckoned Jodie had probably informed her to be on her guard.

No, it would just be a waiting game. Most people go out at some point during the day.

And she did. It just so happened that she did so whilst I was round the corner switching into my Escort. When I got back round to the house I noticed that a blue Corsa, which I had started to suspect might be hers, was now missing and that there were no signs of movement from inside the house. After about an hour and a half, during which time I had started to think about making my move there and then, the car and the woman returned.

196

I studied her as she walked from the car to the front door. She made me think of someone who had lost something. Not in the sense of scrabbling round desperately seeking its return. No. She had the look of someone who knew that, whatever it was she'd lost, it was never coming back. All her remaining energy was spent staying rigid and controlled so that she did not lose anything else – like someone carrying a very full bucket of water.

Don't ask me how I got all that from such a brief and detached acquaintance. Some say I'm fanciful.

Anyway, I called it a day at that. Chances are she wouldn't be off out again today and Morgan was likely to be back in the next couple of hours.

I spent some of the afternoon in the gym and a little of the evening on the phone to Debra. I missed her and it was difficult to create intimacy across the miles apart. Closeness like I had never experienced was there between us whenever we really needed it, but it couldn't be drummed up at will via idle chitchat. Debs suggested that, if I hadn't managed to dig any dirt on Morgan by the weekend, then I should take a couple of days break with her. I whole-heartedly agreed.

The next morning I started off in the Escort. I also waited until around the time that she had popped out the day before. People are creatures of habit. People who give off such an air of rigidity and control are likely to be even more so.

Bingo. When I got there, the Corsa was just pulling away. I reckoned I had a good hour and a half of snooping ahead of me. I kept moving, made a circuit of the block and came back, cheekily pulling into the driveway of chez Morgan.

I aimed my Escort straight at the garage and pressed the button on the handset as I eased up to it in first. The door clicked, whirled, and began its smooth ascent into the recess in the garage ceiling. I'd soon find out if Jodie was still in by crashing into the back of her car. Nope. The garage was empty and the door started to travel back down slowly behind me once I was fully in and had killed the engine. There was plenty of room for me to open the car door and step out, given that my car ain't as wide as a Merc. I had the luxury of not having to deal with the alarm just yet, so I snooped around inside the garage for a bit. Nothing of note. The usual household utilities and cleaning products.

The door from garage to kitchen was locked but gave it up fine to my credit card. Flimsy enough to have kicked it in but, although I wasn't bothered whether they'd know I'd been in, I wanted to avoid the 'breaking' part of breaking and entering if at all possible.

The alarm sensor in the kitchen triggered when I was halfway to the next door. A loud 'Whoop whoop whoop' then a very brief pause before sounding again. The third set of whoops were only just starting by the time I'd made it down the hall, seen the alarm panel and the wire leading from it, and ripped the plug from its socket – silencing the damn thing.

I was relying on that fact that alarms go off briefly all the time and that no bugger wants to get involved anyway. Even if I got a concerned knock at the door, I knew enough about the resident to spin a yarn as to why I had a legitimate reason to be there. Long lost cousin or something. On the handsome side of the family.

I was all set to work my way around the house. Quickly and semi-methodically. I was hoping for anything that might be incriminating or even just illuminating. If Jodie Morgan was in the business of purposefully abusing her clients then maybe she kept her own personal-reflective-wank-diary-journal to get off on. Maybe even 'souvenirs' from her clients as symbols of her power over them – not that I'd know any if I saw them.

The downstairs was neat, tidy – anally retentive. It was all relatively new in terms of decor. Dark woods and creamy soft furnishings. Ash coloured laminate flooring with a large, luxurious one-tone rug the dusty colour of paprika that has lost its freshness. I didn't like it. Along one wall a low rosewood bookshelf held works of women's literature. Austen, Bronte, Carter, Dickinson, Eliot – alphabetically arranged.

I didn't linger too long. I wanted to start with wherever it was she did her paperwork and then branch out from there.

In the 'study' upstairs, the books were more to do with therapy and gender studies. Lots of stuff on feminist interpretations of Freud, recent publications on working with survivors of sexual and ritual abuse, False Memory Syndrome, the obligatory Simone De Beauvoir, the less than obligatory Naomi Wolf, and then a dalliance with the works of Michel Foucault and Jean Baudrillard.

I was beginning, despite myself, to be

impressed. Perhaps we'd have a decent conversation if ever I confronted her.

Then I noticed an extensive collection of the works of the Marquis de Sade, including four different copies of *Justine* – ranging from a turn of the century leather-bound collector's item to an illustrated 1997 version in Spanish. Well, I flicked through it, didn't I? Good artwork. They'd managed to make the poor lass look like she was actually enjoying herself. But, the thinking woman's pornography notwithstanding, I'd noticed there was something odd about her book collection, both upstairs and downstairs. There was none of the mishmash of well-thumbed, dog-eared favourites. No second hand, fifty-pence-a-throw penguins with their blue spines and their *cafe au lait* pages. Most people's book collections start out on a shoestring as a teenager or student and build up gradually – as ideals change and bank balances grow. They contain clues about not only who the person is, but also what they want to be, and – often most telling of all – where they came from to start with.

Jodie Morgan's books were all pristine. I flicked a few open at random – all new, even the old classics had been reprinted within the last few years. Her books were not companions she had carried with her for years. They were recent decorations. Brand labels. Make up. As if she were trying to construct a self-image, using the books as signifiers. Trying to convince herself or others that she was what she said she was – a proper feminist, a therapist, an intellectual.

Well she wasn't fooling me. She was a jumped up little Hitler. Perhaps she'd only bought Foucault and Baudrillard because they sounded like girl's names.

Her PC was set up in the study. That would be worth a look, not everyone bothers to enable a password. But then I noticed a floor safe under her desk – just a heavy metal box, not set in concrete or anything, but beyond the lugging capacity of an opportunist thief. It had a circular dial with a number pad on it. This was potentially the most interesting item. Not something everyone has in their home.

I scrabbled around for some utility bills, finance agreements, whatever. Soon found her home telephone number, bank account number, sort code and date of birth. There were also a few business cards with her office and mobile number. I was going to work on the basis that we are a four-digit

PIN society, and also my assertion that the mass of men lead lives of scant imagination.

After only about a minute and a half of busking, the safe yielded to the first four digits of her office phone number. B,i,n,g,o and Bingo was his name-o.

Life isn't always like that but, if you follow the Dao, it'll kick in when you need it most.

I didn't like what I found.

I don't have a problem with pornography. I tend to think that anything that goes on between two or more consenting adults is fine. I also tend to think that it's fine for those adults to fantasise about and visually depict whatever the hell they like as long as they keep a clear boundary between fantasy and reality.

Jodie Morgan had crossed that boundary.

I can't really describe the stuff. She'd taken the 'damsel in distress' concept and made it her own. She liked her women broken. There was little of the regular bondage type stuff. She had photos of what could only be described as 'war crimes'. In amongst all this there was a stack of legitimate papers from Her Majesty's Stationary Office – inquests and public enquiries – detailing various instances of suicide by young women. I was familiar enough with each case to know that they were all against a background of systematic abuse, poverty, failure of health and social services to help, and plain old bad luck. I flicked through to see if Ms. Morgan appeared to have a personal connection to any of these cases but none jumped out at me.

They must just have been light reading for her.

Then I found some of her own writing. She had produced reams of poorly constructed literature that resembled 'Cinderella' but without the happy ending.

This could explain her move into a therapeutic profession. Access to the vulnerable for the purposes of her own sexual gratification.

A single piece of paper fell to the floor from amongst the stack of filth I was holding. It was a warm spring day and the house was centrally heated yet I shivered as I picked it up. My spine felt like a brittle icicle, which threatened to shatter as I read her sick words.

You are worthless. All of you. You have been raped by your fathers, your brothers, your boyfriends and husbands. Now you are my babies to play with.

That bitch.

But how would such a person be allowed to practise? Surely the process of her training and supervision would lead someone to have suspicions about her motives? How could her employers let her get away with it?

The next thing I found answered my questions.

At the back of the safe was one of those brown A4 envelopes with the cardboard back. It had 'do not bend' printed on it in red ink. Normally they contain certificates or photos. This contained the latter.

Taken from what looked like a hidden position halfway up a wall, there were several photos of a man I recognised.

It was the Chief Executive of the Bradford Health Trust.

He was sat on a rug, wearing a nappy and eating shit.

A glance back through the series of pictures confirmed the shit as being his own.

As this was probably not an activity he listed in the hobbies and interests section of his CV, I leapt to the fairly obvious conclusion that Jodie Morgan was blackmailing him.

It would explain the sudden career change, and I'd been wondering about the Merc and all the home furnishings on a therapist's salary.

I pocketed those photos and I left. Didn't need anything else.

I got home and took the longest fucking shower of my life.

22

Salma Mallinson let out a deep breath, pushed it out, almost as a groan, and stretched out on the sofa. She examined the ceiling above her. Intricate, colourful winding ivy had been painted there. Not stencilled – painted. It was beautiful and it made her smile.

'Under the ivy,' she said quietly, sighing again. She turned to Susie and smiled again.

Susie smiled back.

'This house makes me smile,' Salma explained.

'Thank you. You're not the first who's said that.'

'Bet I won't be the last either. It's like a sanctuary.'

'Something we all need at times.'

'I wish hospital was more like this.'

'Perhaps then it wouldn't be hospital.'

'You're right. Hospitals shouldn't be too pleasant. You've got to *want* to leave.'

'You wanted to leave, and you did,' stated Susie.

'Three cheers for Salma!' the girl giggled triumphantly.

'Have as many as you want. This is sanctuary. No cheer limit.'

'Hoo-ray for Mall-in-son!' she sang Mallinson as if it were 'Hollywood'.

'You were on the ward the same time as Linzi, weren't you?'

'I was. Poor Linzi. They messed with her head. Tried to make her forget who she was.'

'Salma. Is it okay if I ask you some things about her?'

'Of course it is. But is it okay if I cry a lot?'

'No Kleenex limit here either,' smiled Susie.

Salma Mallinson was what psychiatrists called 'labile'. She had mood swings. Call it a chemical imbalance if you want but, if you knew some of the things she'd had to deal with in her life and the ghosts of those things that still clung, you'd consider her mood swings understandable. Sometimes it became too much for her and she would ask to go into hospital. Sometimes, it became too much for others and she would be told to go into hospital. Right now, she felt well enough to cope. She'd been off her lithium for a while now and felt better for it. Less sluggish and bloated. She'd spent her time in hospital proving to the staff and her consultant that she could take the rough with the smooth and just ingest some neuroleptics as and when she needed.

Salma had taken her own discharge the day before Linzi ended up on observations for the last time. She'd wondered, in the self-punishing way that people do, whether the loss of an ally had been one of the things that had pushed Linzi to the edge. But she brought herself up short. She'd considered, even attempted, suicide enough times to know that it was a very personal choice – very little to do with what anyone else was doing or thinking at the time.

If she was honest, she probably really wasn't an ally. She liked to think that of herself – the patient's patient – but she remembered Linzi as being too screwed up, too suspicious, too intent on holding on to her own truth to let anyone else in – lest they implant their own polluting thoughts – or even present a well meaning distraction that robbed her of her focus, her power.

A distressed person is, in essence, someone holding onto the last bit of power that they can.

'Towards the end, she really wanted to be called Morgan. She thought it was a way of protecting the real her. She said that the person they were treating wasn't the real Linzi. Well, that just sounded mad to them, didn't it? But I knew what she meant.'

'You understood her resistance...' reflected Susie.

'She'd been through shit. She watched her parents die. They were good people, she said. Not like mine. Shit, told you I might start crying, didn't I?'

'It's OK.'

Salma collected herself a little before continuing, tears still in her eyes.

'She watched them die, but no one wanted to help her with that. They wanted to know about her husband abusing her. She'd dealt with that. She didn't want to go there. But they made her. The therapist made her.'

'She spoke with you about the pressure she was under?'

'You could see the pressure she was under. She'd come back from therapy sessions heartbroken. Absolutely heartbroken. She'd talk to me about it then. Soon she started to come back angry. Silent, mostly. Then she'd start to smash things, cut up. That's when they really started dosing her.'

'What was happening for Linzi?'

'The therapist wanted to hear about the things her ex had done to her. She wanted details; stuff that Linzi didn't want to talk about. Then she started making bitchy comments about the nurse that helped her through it.'

'Bitchy comments?'

'This guy, nice guy who really helped her once – that Jodie woman said that he sounded like an abuser. Asked Linzi if he'd taken her to the woods and felt her up. Kept saying "it's okay, you can tell me about it", told her he'd done it to other patients and been sacked for it. Linzi knew it wasn't true but that woman just kept on about it.'

'And the upset turned to anger...'

'Not at that. She was well sad that anyone would say that, but she knew it wasn't true and, besides, she knew the guy could defend himself. She was clever that way. She wouldn't waste her energy. But her dad, he wasn't around to answer back...'

Susie did nothing but raise her eyebrows

210

almost imperceptibly and lean slightly forward.

'That's what sent her over. Being told that her dad had been at it with her too...'

23

When I spoke to Debra that night, she listened with interest and helped me decide my next course of action. She also helped me with something else. With a tenderness that only the strong seem to possess, she made me feel good again. She did it by talking dirty to me. Our kind of dirty. A world away from Jodie Morgan's kind of dirty – but still filth.

I needed it. I imagined that a rape victim, or someone who had been physically disfigured, or even a pregnant woman, might need the same kind of tenderness and the same kind of passion to make them feel that a normal, fulfilling sex life was still their right – that what they had with their partner had not somehow been lost or destroyed because of what they'd gone through.

Anyway, as soon as my sweaty palm had

replaced the receiver I found another use for it. I got a grip of myself. When I said I was no abuser, I wasn't counting self-abuse.

It's the main reason I gave up Catholicism.

Morning. After welcoming the rising sun with some *Qi Gong* breathing exercises, I waited for the school traffic to die down and set about my task. I was off to see the Wizard.

The Chief Executive's name was Herman McIntyre. He did, indeed, appear to be a strange mixture of German and Scottish. Perhaps he had some royal blood. Buggered if I was going to stand on ceremony though. He'd been nominally involved at the time I'd ceased my former employment with the Bradford Health Trust and I hadn't developed a great deal of respect for him back then.

The Trust's headquarters weren't at the Heights. They were across town and commanded an altogether better view of the city. It was a large but not too imposing Victorian building. It had once been a hospital itself – a 'fever hospital' rather than a bin. It had extensive grounds that would once have been dotted with blanket-adorned consumptive patients, dying slowly in the open air – as was the fashion of the day. Now it just had rose bushes and new Volvo estates. A recent sandblasting had robbed it of even more character.

Now, not a single patient darkened its doors. It was home to conference rooms, admin. departments, a couple of community teams and, of course, the top knobs.

The inside could be a bit of a maze to the uninitiated but I knew where to go. As I suspected, the fleshy, beady-eyed secretary was ready for me, gate-keeping McIntyre's inner sanctum. She was the kind of horn-rimmed spectacle librarian type who did her veg shopping in Marks & Spencers. She probably had a drawer full of paper doilies at home too. Me, I had a Pierre Cardin leather jacket and an attitude.

No contest.

'Mr. O'Brien to see Mr. McIntyre,' I said quietly, calmly and with a smile. 'I'm afraid I don't have an appointment,' I added helpfully

'Mr. McIntyre is not available,' said without a smile. Corporate hostility.

'That's okay. I'll wait right here. I'll probably be poor company for you though. I tend to hum in an irritating manner when I'm bored.'

'Mr. McIntyre is not in the building and won't be returning today.'

'Funny. I could swear that's his Jag outside the window...'

She didn't know what to say to this, so she went back to, 'Mr. McIntyre is not available,' but added, 'Please would you leave.'

I sat down on the leather three-seater sofa and began to hum. I almost immediately irritated myself. She fixed me with a hard stare that probably made teenage shop assistants feel like cowering.

'I could call security if you wish...'

I got up and walked over to her desk, leaning across it slightly before I spoke. Think casual rather than threatening.

'Regardless of how much fun I might have resisting my removal, I really do want to see Herman. Perhaps you could give him this...' I produced a small white envelope from my pocket and held it out to her, 'and let him decide whether he wants to see me or not.'

Implying some sort of secret knowledge between her boss and I – reinforced ever so slightly by dropping in his first name – she couldn't really refuse, at the risk of incurring his displeasure at her executive decision. She took the envelope and disappeared into his office.

Inside the envelope was one of my business cards that I had run off on the PC last night. It stated my name and profession as usual but underneath it read: *Grant me an audience to make me happy, or I'll tell everyone you wear a nappy.*

The secretary emerged a few moments later, looking confused and defeated. Yer man, Herman, stuck his head out from behind the thick wooden door and jerked his neck at me in a no nonsense 'you'd better come in, hadn't you?' sort of gesture.

'Do I know you?' he asked with furrowed brow, once I was safely behind the closed door.

'Can't expect you to remember everyone you sack...' I shrugged.

He hadn't actually sacked me. I'd claimed, and proved, and been awarded compensation for, constructive dismissal – but it didn't roll off the tongue as easy.

'Is that what this is about?'

'Not at all. This is about these...'

I took the brown envelope of photos out from under my jacket and threw them onto his desk.

'...and it's about Jodie Morgan.'

He had already swooped and descended on the photos, thumbing quickly through them to check their authenticity. His tone changed from reproach and fear to collusion and hope as he urgently spat out his words.

'Where did you get these?'

'Morgan's house.'

'Does she have copies? Is this the only set?'

'I'd imagine there are more. She'd have been a fool not to have made copies, or at least kept the negatives.'

'Could you get those too? I can pay you. I just want an end to all this,' he shook his head as if he were trying to shake off a buzzing insect. Sweat formed on his temples.

'Herman, I don't really care what you want. What I want is for you to deal with Jodie Morgan. She's abusing her clients and you're her employer. Morgan's idea of 'therapy' is what led to Linzi Delaney's death. You shouldn't be letting this happen.'

'I know what she's doing. I know it's wrong. I've had to get rid of other employees who have spoken out against her. Good people. People I'd worked with for years. You can see the hold she has over me, for God's sake.'

He was shouting now. I wondered if Doily could hear through the door.

'That's your problem and I don't propose

to solve it for you. All I'm saying is that you should put a stop to her. If you don't, I will. Believe me, I will really go to town on her and the blackmail won't be left out.'

'Can't you? Leave it out I mean?'

'No. If you want to investigate her, report her, run her over in your bloody Jag – then do it. Work it out yourself. I don't want to waste another moment bothering myself with this shit. It's your job. I'm giving you, as her boss, the chance to do the right thing. If you can find a way of leaving your sex life out of it, then fine. If not, then I'm using everything I've got on her.'

'I can't. I just can't.'

He collapsed into his plush leather chair. He looked small, old and weary. He stared into space for a long while, and then looked up at me with pleading eyes. He looked pathetic, even without the nappy.

'What can I do? I have a wife and family, a career...'

'And golf club membership, no doubt. Look Herman, what you do in your spare time isn't anything other than embarrassing. It's not illegal. It's not immoral. You're not hurting anyone. It's a fetish. A hobby. It's not a lot different to stamp collecting. Don't worry about that. If you've been giving her money out of your own pocket then you're a fool. If you've been shaving it off your budget somehow then you're a fool who's out of a job. All this *will* come out. Save face. Redeem yourself by doing the right thing. You cannot allow Jodie Morgan to stay in her position. You cannot let her get away with treating people like that.'

He wasn't looking at me. He wasn't really looking at anything. I decided to leave. I turned to him as I got to the door.

'Do something. Or I will.'

In case he hadn't got the message already. Still no response.

I left, with the sinking feeling that I was going to have to do the doing myself.

I spent the afternoon playing pool with Kelp. Trying to feel normal again. Winning every match helped. So did several bottles of *Zywiec*. I'd give Herman a few days and I'd check back in on him. See what he'd done. Perhaps I should get myself down to London in the meantime. I needed something to take my mind off it all.

Didn't realise that was just what I was about to get.

24

Sat at home, after a meal of polenta, bacon, green beans and a bottle of EB Pils, watching telly. My mobile rang. It was Val Townley, the copper from South London. We exchanged greetings.

'I called your office first, didn't want to disturb you in the middle of something. Where are you?' she asked.

'Back up North now, and all the better for it, thank you.'

'Are you alone?'

'Except for my cat. Why?'

'I've got some sensitive info to pass onto you, didn't want to put you in a difficult position if you were with anyone.

'Oh. Is this one of those "are you sitting down" moments?'

'Fraid so, O'Brien.'

'Has there been another assault?'

'A killing. A brutal killing. We've got some experienced officers down here but it's shook us all up.'

I felt my muscles tighten, then shudder

with an almost electrical charge as the hair follicles along my bare arms contracted. An evolutionary leftover. An animal response to perceived threat.

'Geoffrey? Did they get to Geoffrey Sitcha?' I swallowed hard after the sentence as my mouth had dried during the speaking of it.

'No, O'Brien. It was Jonathon Pasloe. I'm sorry.'

'What happened?'

'We don't know. We hadn't made any contact with him. He called me last Saturday, started to try and tell me about something that was going to go down. Asked for your number but I wouldn't give it. I tried to set up a meeting but he rang off in panic. It was the last we heard. Found his body this morning.'

'How was he killed?'

'You don't want to know.'

'Tell me.' For some reason it seemed important.

'Don't be a ghoul.'

'Val. I presume his death was meant to be some kind of statement. I got involved in this, I feel like I should know.'

'That's the reason I did you the courtesy of calling you, not to give you the gory details.'

'Even so...'

Val sighed. She tried to keep it matter of fact but there was anger in her voice. I guess some of it was at me.

Jonathon Pasloe, she told me, had been beaten to death with hammers. Multiple assailants. Multiple hammers. Actually, they weren't sure if the beating itself killed him. He may still have been alive when they started nailing him to a wooden partition wall of an abandoned flat where his body was found. The six-inch nails were hammered through his wrists, forearms, ankles, testicles and ear lobes. His tongue had been torn out or, rather, torn to pieces as they tried to remove it – a pair of pliers not being a particularly precise surgical instrument. The largest remaining piece had been nailed to his forehead in what one would expect was a clumsy symbolism of his betrayal.

They knew from defence wounds on his forearms that he had tried in vain to shield himself from some of the blows – so they at least knew the beating had come first. What they couldn't tell was whether he had been made to watch as they nailed his pet dog halfway up the opposite wall, or whether it had just been done as an afterthought.

John's girlfriend had reported him missing

on the Sunday night. On Monday morning, she received an envelope full of Polaroid photographs showing both mutilated bodies from various angles. The envelope had been addressed to their five-year-old daughter and they had sat and opened it together.

By the time the police found Jonathon and the dog, they had been dead for around 48 hours. Being nailed to the wall at least meant that it was only John's feet that were missing – the neighbourhood rats were still chewing on the tattered, fleshy stumps when the first officers got there. They scattered off into the splintered, rotting floor as soon as the torches were shined on them, their plump bodies and thrashing tails colliding with each other in the rush. The flies and cockroaches were harder to get rid of. Their noise alone was enough to make you vomit and, if you did, you just try keeping them away from your own face.

It was a nightmare. Val had spent much of the afternoon persuading one of the officers who had been first to arrive that he should take some sick leave. He had wanted to resign.

She said she had just heard in the last half hour that John's girlfriend was in hospital following a massive overdose. The little girl had been taken into care but was likely to end up in hospital too. She had not slept, eaten, drunk or even spoken a word since Monday morning.

'I'm sorry, Val.'

'For what happened or for making me tell you?'

'Both. I'm sorry.'

'OK.'

'Have you arrested anyone?'

'No. All the usual suspects have disappeared without trace. No one's talking to us.'

'What did John say before he got scared off?'

'Not a lot. He sounded coked up. Said "they'd got together". Said they "were planning to really do it". I asked who "they" were, he just said "the other blokes". I asked when "it" was planned to happen. That's when he panicked, like someone was going to hear him. The last thing he said was "It's OK. See you Sunday." That was it.'

'Sunday? Sunday's gone. Anything happen Sunday?'

'Apart from Pasloe's murder, you mean?'

'Sorry. It just sounds to me like he was trying to tip you off...'

'Me too.'

'But not about his own murder...'

'Wasn't my impression either.'

'So, you're not aware of any other attacks?'

'No. All quiet. Too quiet.'

'Maybe we're barking up the wrong tree with the Sunday thing. Maybe he was just saying the first thing that came into his head.'

'Well, O'Brien. Just thought I'd let you know.'

'Cheers, Val. How's the investigation going?'

'We got search warrants for all Pasloe's known associates. Nothing doing. We've got a massive police presence in Thamesmead.'

'Is that achieving anything?'

'Only the growing realisation that none of those bastards are anywhere in or near Thamesmead.'

'I should come down. I should do something.'

'Like what?' She sounded tired and angry. But there was a tiny hint of compassion in there too.

'I don't know. I could go talk to his girlfriend or something...'

'Don't be ridiculous! What on earth would she want from you right now?'

'You're right. I'm sorry. I just want to help

if I can.'

'Look, you take care, O'Brien. You're a good man, but that doesn't exactly count for a lot these days, I'm sorry to say. Try not to lose any sleep over it. Nice meeting you. Bye.'

And she was gone.

I felt deflated. I didn't feel the righteous anger and the need to do something that Geoffrey's beating and Linzi's death had stirred in me. I guess I felt afraid. Despite feeling bad about what had happened I didn't really want to get involved. I'd been scared before but it had always been over-taken by other sets of feelings or beliefs. For the first time since choosing my sometimes violent and often seedy profession, I wanted out. I didn't want to be part of a world where people got nailed to walls.

I drifted off into an uneasy sleep. It was weird. It was only early evening for a start, I was still in the armchair and the cat was still on my lap. I don't normally nod off after a distressing phone call, but as I tried to distance myself from the images Val had given me, I sort of felt pulled away from reality. I dreamt I was fighting a battle against seemingly impossible odds but carried on, knowing that I had right on my side.

The imagery in my head was from some

books I had read when I was young. *The Chronicles of Narnia* by C.S. Lewis. I was alone. I was amongst allies but still alone. I was seeking members of my war counsel. I needed help and advice. Sword drawn, I walked quickly and nervously, stumbling through woods and fields, looking for help. Every talking beast I passed, every faun, satyr and centaur said the same thing. 'They've captured Aslan's How.' Finally, tired and cold and hungry, I found who I was looking for. The wise old half-dwarf, pale yet magical in the moonlight, said to me 'gather your greatest warriors. We must draw them out.'

I awoke with a start, the telly still on but turned down low from when I'd been on the phone. Cat still on my lap. I looked at it as if it had some answers. It looked back at me as if I was wrong.

Aslan's How. The monument to the Great Lion. It seemed daft, but I'm from a Celtic tradition and dreams have always been there for us to sort that kind of shit out.

'That Polish lager...' I said to the cat.

I checked my mobile. The received call had a number. I rang it back.

'Val Townley...'

'Val, hi. You know when you told me about

the attempted murder of Geoffrey Sitcha?'

'Yeah?'

'You said it seemed like a copycat beating. Like some stuff that had happened somewhere else.'

'Yeah. The Lion Estate. New Cross. Why?'

'That's where they're holed up. That's who they've got together with.'

'How do you know?'

'I had a dream.'

She snorted. 'You and Martin Luther King. Look where it got him.'

'What do you reckon?'

'It's plausible. In fact, we'll look into it. I won't be able to divert many resources unless I can come up with some sort of argument, and that place is what you'd call a no-go area.'

'Didn't believe there was any such thing.'

'Not to us there isn't, but you won't get ambulances or fire engines there – not without a police escort and, believe me, I don't blame them. We don't have a beat there, just go in mob-handed when we think we need to.'

'Val, it's been nice talking again. I think I might see you soon,' I said before hanging up.

I arose from my chair and checked the

clock. 10.08pm. I wasn't feeling scared anymore. Time to go to work.

Got to go gather my greatest warriors.

25

I didn't feel tired now but I had a quick coffee anyway just to give my nervous system a bit of a tweak. As I sipped at it, I recalled my conversation with Asif. I had been quite insistent that all my actions were through choice, but now I was beginning to wonder. Not much more than an hour ago, I had admitted to myself that all this was too much for me. It scared the shit out of me and I didn't want to get involved. There was no one putting pressure on me, nobody crying for my help. But, all of a sudden, I was obligated. I was on course for a showdown and feeling strangely serene about it. Sometimes I get that feeling, like I'm running on rails. A predetermined path. I tended to trust this feeling. It didn't take fear away, just made it matter a little less.

Large Benny told me he didn't know what fear was. He also told me he'd never experienced racism. He insisted that he was too big and scary for people to be anything other than extremely polite and deferential to him. He had a point. He was exaggerating, of course, but only the very, very drunk were ever silly enough to challenge or insult him. Rare occurrence but, as it happens, one that I was witness to as I got to the door of Zeds that night.

It was a Wednesday night so there was no queue at the door and minimal staffing. Wednesdays were always quiet in terms of numbers but not necessarily trouble free. Slow drinking students would make use of the free entry, cheaper drinks, and proximity to the University. Those who still had any giro left from the day before would also descend for roughly the same reasons, but with the additional reason of twatting a student.

Despite this scenario, actual violence rarely materialised. The punters were so thin on the ground and so bloody obvious in their actions, that fisticuffs were normally headed off at the pass.

As I walked down from one end of the street towards Zeds I could see and hear a group of four lads coming up the other way. I could hear them because their language was excessively loud and colourful.

'1 hope that big fat black nigger in't in tonight,' said one of them. Audible from further up the street so they were certainly announcing their presence to whoever was on the door. Unless it was Danny, the ex-Para with his own racist views that he barely managed to keep in check around the rest of us, then these lads were ending their night early.

'Fuck 'im. There's four of us,' replied his mate. The ability to count remaining with him even though he had quite obviously lost the power of reason.

I was about to quicken my pace and head them off myself, when I saw a shadow the size of the former Yugoslavia looming just inside the doorway. I smiled and actually slowed my pace a little – hang back and watch.

The guys turned into the doorway without modifying their pace – as if they were merely turning the corner of a street and it was irrelevant to them whether anyone would be in their way.

They literally *bounced* off Large Benny.

He stared down at them. He had perfected a stare that was not so much threatening as crushing. He could look at you as if you meant absolutely nothing. These guys were less significant than dogshit to him. Dogshit at least arouses displeasure. None of them could appreciate it or articulate what it meant, but Large Benny had provided them all with a moment of existential enlightenment. His *Being* threw their *Nothingness* into bold relief. Like wondering stiff-necked at a star-filled sky on a clear silent night. It was a wonderful gift for him to give.

All they could do in return was mutter expletives. Ungracious bastards.

'Bigfatblacknigger...' mumbled the guy who had been virtually yelling the same words a little earlier.

They had bounced back far enough to be out of arm's reach; they'd indulge in a bit of verbal from this distance before skulking off. They didn't know I was now standing behind them though.

'Two tautologies in one sentence. Way to go,' I piped up.

The lads spun their heads to me then quickly back to Large Benny, checking that he hadn't moved forward.

'Eh?' said the guy.

'Fat implies big and nigger implies black – thus rendering half your sentence redundant,' I explained.

'You're talking absolute shite,' chipped in Large Benny.

'That's another way of putting it,' I agreed, as the lads started to slope off – galvanised into action by the sound of Large Benny's raspy baritone. He turned towards me and smiled.

'I was talking to you, OB,' he explained.

We had a chat. I told Benny that I was putting together a posse and heading down to London to front up with some nazi scum. He said it sounded fun but that he would have to check with the boss, Tim Marconi, whether it was okay as he had been due to work the weekend.

'When I tell him I'm working for you, I'm sure he'll roll over,' he added. 'Tim thinks the sun shines out of your arse.'

From the club office, I phoned Debra and explained that I was coming down. Naturally she was up for it and she assured me that Geoffrey Sitcha would be too.

The only other person I was going to have any joy with tonight was Bic, so I gave him a call. I knew him from my kung fu class. He could outdo any of us in the training exercises that we did and was very difficult to get one over on in sparring. He insisted that he'd never been in a real fight in his life.

Thing is, he was quite keen for it to happen but wasn't the kind of guy who'd start it. I thought this might be the time for him to test his skills. The nazi bit definitely swung him. He can't stand them. Bic is a Polish Jew by heritage.

If you're starting to think that I don't know any straight, white, English Protestants – then you're probably right. This is Bradford. They tend to keep themselves to themselves and not bother anyone.

I got some sleep. Thankfully, the talking beasts of Narnia made no further guest appearances.

Thursday morning I plucked up the courage to phone Javeed Ali in Manchester. He had got in touch a little while back to congratulate me on getting myself in the papers. He'd said it was always a pleasure to hear that yet another drug pusher had been removed from the streets. I'd said that it must be nice for him to know that there was one less person out there to compete with. He'd laughed.

I still had his number. He recognised me right away.

'*Alaikum-salaam*, O'Brien. To what do I owe the pleasure?'

'I'd like to speak to Nassir, please. He may

be able to help me with something, if you permit him. First off, do I have your permission to ask?'

These gangsters. They love that 'respect' shit.

With great pride and satisfaction in his voice, Javeed said he was handing the phone over.

'Nassir...' grumbled a bear-like voice from a bear-like man.

I outlined the situation. I think I'd developed quite a sales patter since yesterday. He didn't sound unenthusiastic. A few background mumblings and he came back on the line.

'It's okay with the boss. How much you paying?'

'I was hoping that fun and righteousness were the main rewards, but I'm quite prepared to cover any loss of earnings.'

'£150 a day'll do it.'

A done deal. Good job I still had the majority of Geoffrey's wad. Nassir arranged to meet me in Bradford later in the day, taking the opportunity to pop in on some family too.

I must be slipping. Kelp had popped round and got wind of what I was setting up. He'd badgered and badgered me to let him come and I'd relented. It would be good for him to see his sister but I made him agree that he would stay well clear of any trouble. He'd shot straight home to pack a bag and turned up a little later with a full rucksack.

'What you got there? Anti-aircraft gun?'

He just smiled enigmatically. That should have worried me, but I let it go.

Large Benny turned up around lunchtime. Tim was with him.

'Have you come to tell me off for nicking one of your staff?' I asked.

'Fuckin' comin' with you, aren't I?' he replied.

I was pleased. Tim wasn't much bigger than one of Large Benny's legs, but he was about the most dangerous man I knew. Possibly almost as dangerous as my girlfriend. God, I move in some strange circles.

Bic was close behind them, looking impossibly handsome and not how you'd imagine a fighter. But self-confidence oozed out of him and he was soon one of the lads. Nassir turned up last and I did the introductions. He only had to tilt his head up a fraction to meet Large Benny's eyes. Nassir was quite capable of the 'you're nothing' look and, for a moment, I was worried that they'd test it out on each other. Naa, they nodded at each other like they were in the same club. Brothers by virtue of their size.

I hadn't really thought about transport. We'd all, except Kelp, turned up in separate cars. Together, we might stem the rising tide of Fascism but we were likely to severely knack the environment in the process. There's a place off Leeds Road where I've hired minibuses before so I suggested that. Large Benny had, however, turned up in his very own transit van and it seemed silly not to use it.

Okay, so there were no windows to look out of. We were hard men. We could cope.

It was around 3.30pm when we hit the road. Sat in a metal box with a bunch of heavies. I tried not to think of a similar situation two weeks ago.

It was around 5.45pm when we rolled to a halt on the hard shoulder amidst a clamour of gruff-voiced consternation. Hazard lights flashing and the front of the transit doing a good impression of having been hit by exocet missile.

We all sat on the verge a little way from the van, in case it burst into flames. Large Benny sat staring into space, a mixture of annoyance and guilt etched on his face. Tim, who fancied himself as a bit of an amateur mechanic, was edging back towards the vehicle for a look but I reckoned it would be a while yet. You could still feel the heat from it. I looked at Tim hopefully but he shook his head and sucked air through his teeth. Just like a proper mechanic.

At that moment, my eyes picked up a bright, fast-moving, southbound object heading towards us and my brain told me to keep looking. It was a pink VW camper van. I briefly caught the eyes of the driver as the van sped past. As it did, I was treated to the benign smiling faces of Dorothy, Toto, The Tin man, The Scarecrow and the cowardly Lion.

With a lightening of my heavy heart, I watched the red brake lights come on and the orange left indicator wink on and off. The van pulled onto the hard shoulder up ahead of us.

Saved by the Flying Monkey.

26

I motioned for the lads to grab their gear and follow me.

'What's all this then?' enquired Tim.

'Mates of mine,' I replied.

It did not take the lads long to work out that we had been rescued by a couple of lesbians.

One or two of them seemed a little uncomfortable. I, however, felt eminently comfortable. I'd go so far as to say I'd never travelled in a vehicle so comfortable. This was a far cry from an unvarnished wooden bench resting across a wheel arch. This van had scatter cushions. This van had chuffing *drapes*.

Susie's partner was someone I hadn't met. A cute Asian girl with big brown eyes and several facial piercings, whose body was a pleasing mixture of waif and athlete. Whilst we were chatting she explained she was a Sikh by birth but had been disowned by her family. She now called herself Freya. I managed to catch a look of what could only be described as distaste in Nassir's eyes as he earwigged but said nothing.

From what I had experienced, the cultural values of Sikh and Muslim communities remained pretty similar. Stuff about family and duty and honour had little to do with religion itself, and sometimes even less to do with morality. I reckoned that, leg breaker and drug dealer though he was, Nassir was probably still 'the Big Man' in his family and community. He was likely to be looking down on Freya right now for breaking away from all that, no matter how valid her reasons might be.

The rest of it was just plain embarrassment. This group of desperadoes no longer felt in control of their own destiny. Large Benny, no longer in the driving seat, looked distinctly odd crammed in amongst the soft furnishings. As conspicuous as a tarantula on a French fancy.

Anyway, we were getting a lift, weren't we? Sod their hang-ups.

Kelp was down with it though, and the ladies were taking a shine to him and the puppy dog kind of way he had about him. I smiled to myself as I watched a little seed growing in his mind that he might somehow be in with a chance.

After a while, the ice did seem to be starting to melt. At least the lads were talking amongst themselves whereas before they'd been silent.

I took the opportunity to talk to Susie about the whole Jodie Morgan thing. She didn't seem at all surprised at the blackmail. She told me that, basically, Morgan was a powercrazed bitch. She liked to victimise others. Since women resided most definitely within the more disempowered half of society, they were an obvious choice for her attentions. It had nothing to do with a loving sexual preference. Susie had been talking to people about Morgan and did not like what she had heard. Suffice it to say that, as far as I'm concerned, Jodie Morgan killed Linzi Delaney. She filled her head full of pain and lies to the point where death was the only way of escape. The only way of taking the power back.

Then I asked Susie how come she was heading down to London.

'We're involved in some performance art. New Cross "Joys of Spring" community festival.'

'New Cross? No shit. How 'bout that?'

I told her what we were up to. The lads' ears pricked up and I started to get a growing feeling that we were becoming a proper group – the eight of us there in that van. I told her that we didn't know yet exactly how we were going to do what we wanted to do. Flush them out. Goad them into action. Somehow.

'Put on some street theatre. Fascists hate street theatre,' explained Freya matter of factly.

'We've had some threats about the stuff we're putting on on Sunday,' said Susie.

'Sunday? New Cross?'

Was this what Jonathon Pasloe had been on about?

'It's the biggest gathering that Lesbian And Black Integrated Arts has put on anywhere. There's going to be a rally, a street party – everything.'

I was getting the distinct feeling that this might be the kind of happening that a bunch of Nazis might object to. Violently object to. In areas where black youth culture had too strong a hold for a direct fascist assault, gays were the favoured target. Unite and fight the Batty man.

What we clearly had to do was draw them into some sort of confrontation to pre-empt whatever they had planned – for Sunday or whenever. I asked Freya again about fascists

241

hating street theatre. She took a deep breath.

'Look, most of the performance art you've ever seen has been a bit on the crap side, hasn't it?'

'Yes. I suppose so.'

'It's supposed to be. It's different by its very nature. It strives to be odd. Edgy. Outside. Other. It's unashamed in its indulgence. Fascism is about conformity and about picking on the oddest common denominator. Put on some street theatre, in the middle of this estate, on Saturday and they'll be there like flies on shit.'

'So you think that we...' I waved my hand around to indicate the motley crew, who were now listening intently, '...should put on some sort of outdoor performance?'

'Yeah. And make it as rubbish as possible.'

'Shouldn't be difficult...' mumbled Tim.

I could see that Susie was suppressing a great deal of laughter. Freya just kept looking ahead out of the window. Deadpan and serious and quite possibly taking the piss.

But the more I thought about it, the more reasonable it seemed. I had been working on the basis that we were just going to roam the estate looking for trouble. If we let the trouble come looking for us, we had less chance of being deliberately directed up some blind alleys and we gained an element of surprise. I put it to the group. They were moved to neither praise nor criticism.

'You're the boss,' said Nassir.

'Now look, I'm a Middle Class White Heterosexual Male. I hardly think it's appropriate for me to be the designated leader of such a diverse group,' I challenged.

There were murmurs of both approval and derision.

'Well I'm an Unemployed, Working Class Black, do I get to be boss?' said Kelp.

'Too straight and too male,' said Susie.

'That's got to be the nicest thing anyone's ever said about me,' beamed Kelp.

There was silence for a while, save for the hum of the tyres as we rolled south.

'I think it's going to have to be me,' sighed Freya, her back still to the rest of us.

'Makes sense,' I agreed. 'An Asian lesbian. How much more disenfranchised can you get? I trust you're vilified within your own community as well as by society at large?'

'You bet your ass.'

'Cool.'

'Oh, it gets better. I'm also disabled.'

With that she swung her left leg deftly up

onto the dash and slid up the leg of her grey sweat pants to reveal a prosthetic lower limb.

This drew a round of applause from the assembly and I was glad they were getting into the spirit of it.

'We'll help, of course,' said Freya, looking over at Susie for confirmation and briefly holding hands over the gear stick.

'I don't expect it. I'm sure you've got other things you could be doing. Besides, this could get dangerous.'

'Look OB, these things can get dangerous anyway. We've got experience of that. All our stuff is sorted out already. It would be a pleasure to hang out with you guys for a couple of days and help you with your "performance".'

'Much appreciated then, Suse. I get the feeling you two are enjoying this?'

'The absurdity of it appeals to us,' explained Freya, 'we are political artists but, first and foremost, we are Absurdists.'

'What, like Gilbert and George?'

'Hmm, more like Seigfreid and Roy,' offered Freya.

'Like that, but with fannies,' said Susie.

It soon got mentioned, in the course of general chat, that Susie and Freya had met at a dance class and had both got talking about martial arts – Susie practised Tai Chi Chuan and Freya practised *Aikido*. Yes, with one and a half legs. The talking had turned, fairly quickly, to shagging. Not *that* quickly. I think they at least made it out of the dance class.

You could tell that Kelp wanted to jump in on the shagging part but Bic beat him to it with a barrage of excited questions about their martial arts. It turned into a conversation about the relative merits of the 'hard' and the 'soft' arts, then into a discussion about trained fighters and street fighters. Soon everyone was joining in.

And so it was that we arrived in London, laughing and joking as one big group – with two new members.

Another two members joined as soon as we got there. Debs and Geoffrey were waiting for us. Originally, I'd made an impromptu arrangement that we were all going to cram into Geoffrey's tiny flat. Not ideal, but at least there'd be no students earwigging on us. Susie had, however, come up with a better idea. They had the use of an empty dance studio that we could all crash in. Plenty of floor space and, seeing as it was actually in New Cross, closer to the action.

I'd phoned Debs with the location and they'd agreed to meet us there.

I gave Debs a big, big hug and a major kiss. I reckoned we weren't going to get the chance to be alone together in the next 48 hours at least so I tacked a good two-handed arse squeeze onto the hug to remind me of what I was missing. She bit into my bottom lip as I did so. I took it like a man.

I've probably mentioned before that Debra is abso-frigging-lutely drop dead gorgeous. Everyone was watching us enviously. Even the girls. *Especially* the girls. Kelp was the only one who wasn't. Being that he was her brother. I think it's been good for Kelp that I'm seeing Debra. Since I met him, he's spent a lot of time wanting to be just like me. The fact that I'm shagging his sister kind of pushes him into broadening his points of reference a little.

We got our sleeping arrangements sorted out and had a brew. It took a couple of kettle-fulls for the ten of us. Mugs in hands, we began to bring Debs and Geoff up to speed and discuss our game plan. We decided that we needed some costumes, something that would cover our faces and prevent us from being recognised until the right moment. Freya suggested Ku Klux

Klan outfits – very easy to knock up from white sheets and would have a strikingly ironic quality too. No one had any political or philosophical objections to this, although Bic looked a little wary – I think that was just the fashion victim in him. Susie assured me that she knew someone who was already kitting out people for their event on Sunday, who would have no problem supplying us with our outfits by Saturday morning, particularly if she could be bunged a few quid. Both myself and Geoffrey spoke at the same time, saying it would be no problem. Large Benny turned to Geoffrey and said, 'Dinner on you tonight then, brother?'

The next thing to discuss was publicity. We had all of tomorrow to plan exactly what we were going to do but it would be good if we could let people know the day before that something was going to be happening in their area. Our group needed an identity that it could put about, even if for one day only. We needed a name.

I turned to Susie, 'What was the name of your organisation again?'

'Lesbian And Black Integrated Arts.'

'L.A.B.I.A?'

'That's the one. Bold, isn't it?'

'Takes some licking...' added Freya.

'I find it quite easy to get my tongue round...' said Kelp supportively.

We all agreed that it made for an eye-catching poster, at least on the lampposts and railings of an affluent suburb. I suspected, though, that most of the residents of the Lion would think it was a resort in Ibiza – or at least need a diagram. I expressed this view to those gathered – explaining that our group required an even bolder and more eye-catching name of its own. One that could adorn flyers and posters that would be scattered in the stairwells and pasted to the corrugated metal shutters of garages and closed down shops. Something that would announce our presence and ensure maximum publicity for our event. There was a silence as everyone pondered my pronouncement. Kelp was the first to break it.

'Got one,' he announced proudly.

All eyes were upon him. He paused long enough to make me say, 'Go on then. What is it?'

'Communities-Under-Nazi-Threat,' he grinned.

I kissed his forehead amidst much gruff cheering. We would get them printed up and distributed first thing tomorrow.

Then it was time to get something to eat.

Geoffrey was indeed quite happy to pay for all of us, but eating together was going to be difficult. It didn't matter though. We were all grown ups and perfectly prepared to break up into smaller groups or go it alone. Debs, Susie and Freya linked arms like school friends and headed somewhere vegan, Bic went *Kosher* and Nassir went *Halal*. Both of them had contacts in the city they were going to drop in on and say 'Hi' to anyway. Paying wasn't an issue because the rest of us ended up in an Italian place just off Oxford Street. Tim was known there and was treated like royalty. None of us had to pay.

I had an endless supply of black olives, a minestrone and a seafood tagliatelle. Washed down with a Sicilian Syrah. I'm not a big fan of white wine at all. Even with seafood I'll tend to have red. Or a Guinness. Guinness is superb with seafood, but it wouldn't quite have fit with the ambience on that occasion.

By one in the morning, most of us met back up at the empty dance studio. Both Bic and Nassir had sent texts to say that they would be with us first thing the next day. Bic had sent his to Freya, obviously taking the bit about her being our leader to heart. Nassir sent his to me. Oh, well. At least they hadn't been at each other's throats yet.

Debs was also conspicuous by her absence. I asked Susie if she knew where she'd got to. She smiled at me.

'She's waiting for you.'

'Where?'

'Outside. In the Flying Monkey.'

'Cheers!' I said, and gave her a hug. I was careful not to press my pelvis against her though, as a certain part of my anatomy had already sprung to a state of readiness.

And then I was off down the stairs – as fast as my tumescence would carry me.

27

8.00am Friday morning and we were waiting for the second kettle to boil to sort us all for coffee. Nassir and Bic had turned up from their sojourns and had both had the excellent idea of bringing breakfast, so we had an assortment of rolls, pastries and falooda to fuel us.

Freya and Susie were talking animatedly with each other about how best to organise us into an all singing, all dancing, kick-ass hit squad. Most of the rest of us sat quietly thinking about, in the cold light of day, just how ridiculous this all sounded. No one put forward any better ideas though.

First cup of coffee over with, the lesbians popped over the road to a local newsagents. Kelp tagged along behind them. Soon they returned with several magic markers, a set of alphabet transfers, a pad of A3 paper for posters and a pad of A5 for flyers. We did a few different ones, for variety, but they all bore the acronym of our group in large letters. Each explained, in much smaller letters underneath, that this stood for 'Communities Under Nazi Threat' and that, through the power of dance and song, we were going to smash fascism and bring harmony to both the Lion Estate and the whole world. We finished some of them off with inept drawings of smiling stick people with frizzy hair, dungarees and Doc Martens.

The newsagent nearly shat himself when the whole lot off us turned up and hung around outside his shop whilst Freya and Susie dashed off a stack of photocopies. I just hoped we'd have a similar effect on our opponents when it came to the crunch.

Suse, quite rightly, did not want to take the Flying Monkey anywhere near the Lion. We were based just over a mile away so we all set off walking as a group.

These were mean streets anyway, but the nearer we got to the outskirts of the estate, the meaner they became. The only school children we could see were confined to the backs of cars. Cars that were driving too fast down residential streets that were too full of parked cars already. Harassed drivers willing their journeys to be over, hoping the traffic kept flowing fast enough to avoid having to stop the car – leaving you vulnerable to gangs of lads who might drag you out, beat you senseless in front of your kids, steal your stereo, plates and whatever money you had on you or whatever expensive trainers your kids were wearing. That scenario may never have happened on this particular street – but you could see that everyone had a look that said they didn't want to be the first.

Not that there weren't young kids walking the streets, but a school uniform to them would have been as alien as anything else out of *Harry Potter*. In an area where the emergency services need an escort, you're hardly going to get many visits from social workers and welfare officers. What chance did these kids have? The ones we passed gave us looks as dirty as their clothes, but there was a respect for our size and number as a group so we didn't get any lip.

Mothers young and old rattled their screeching buggies past us. Pinched faces, hair tied tightly back, acne, dull red eyes, tobacco-yellow fingers, wearing every item of jewellery they owned lest it got stolen. They wore baggy tops with stained leggings that displayed bony white ankles covered with fading scabs and blisters.

There weren't many men on the street. The lucky ones were maybe out on a building site or at some warehouse for a bit of cash in hand. Those without the motivation or social skills for even the most menial labour would all be indoors at this hour either asleep or cracked off their faces. That was the reason that women and kids drifted aimlessly around the streets – avoiding the menfolk.

It became less populated as we got onto the estate proper. It seemed that people only ventured outdoors when they needed to, and walked damn quickly when they did. Anyone exiting one of the three ugly, decaying tower blocks that dominated the centre of the estate had quite a gauntlet to run. Firstly they had to avoid being mugged or molested on the stairs. Then they had to glance skywards to check for any large items of electrical equipment that might be thrown from above. Then they had to brave the packs of roaming dogs and watch for joy riders steaming in and doing handbrake turns that often resulted in rear-ends being smashed against the walls of the tower blocks. If all that happened to you was that you got shit on your shoes you considered it a lucky day.

It really was a mess. Leaking water had stained the concrete blocks with rusty scars. From where I stood, I could see at least two washing machines and three TVs imbedded in the surrounding patches of mud that had not seen a blade of grass since the 70s. The twisted chassis of a cheap saloon car still smelt of burnt plastic and rubber as we walked past it. Everywhere, on mud and tarmac, broken glass glinted in the morning sun – as ubiquitous as dew drops on a fresh pasture, just not as pretty.

If this was indeed where the Nazis were staying then they were welcome to it.

We split into three groups and went round sticking up our posters anywhere we thought they might get some attention. We scattered flyers over the street, on parked or abandoned cars and got ignored when we tried to hand them to people. Some even went into letterboxes. We'd done bloody loads of them.

By 10.45am, we were back in the dance studio. Some of the lads I was with were used to dealing with scary situations and knew how to control their adrenaline. But I bet, like me, they had butterflies in their stomachs right now, as Freya plugged in her ghetto blaster and we all shifted awkwardly from foot to foot, regretting that we'd agreed to this poncey street theatre lark. When the music came on, it welcomingly cut through the uncomfortable silence.

We had a compilation of disco classics on CD, well known to just about everyone. It played in the background as Freya got us loosened up with some callisthenics exercises. If you didn't know about her leg, there's no way you would have been able to tell. She was an amazing dancer.

For those of us who practised martial arts, it wasn't too difficult to make the transition to dance. For those of us who were so big that they didn't need to practise martial arts, it took a little longer. But Freya was a great teacher. She knew how to recognise someone's strengths and how to build on them. How to engender confidence in one's abilities. As we gradually worked our way into the positions Freya wanted us in, Large Benny and Nassir flanked us like huge bookends. Their movements more understated, less fluid, mainly head bobbing and foot tapping with their hands clasped in front of them, but containing us with a certain rhythm. They were enjoying themselves.

We were all enjoying ourselves. The music had been turned up louder. Those 70s sounds had a school disco feel, and it was like we were back in the classroom. Big kids having a laugh. It was like we were putting on a school play and we all wanted to make this thing work. I looked around at this bunch of hard lads starting to camp it up with a sense of abandon. Gay abandon? Blame it on the Boogie.

We'd already bonded well as a group in the last 24 hours but those bonds had taken on a softer quality. Now, that doesn't necessarily mean we were going to have the shit kicked out of us. If you know about martial arts then you'll know that softness means toughness too. Less brittle. Less inclined to break.

By the end of the day we had three dance routines worked out to perfection and were doing group karaoke onto the backing tracks that we would dance to. We were in stitches, rolling on the ground gasping for breath at times, biting our sleeves. Slapping the floor and each other's backs. It was an absolute riot to watch and hear ourselves perform. We had eventually decided on two Village People numbers and one by the Weather Girls.

At the opening piano chords of 'It's Raining Men', Freya would announce on the mike, in a completely serious voice, that this song was dedicated to those members of the conscripted forces in Israel who refused to fight in an unjust war against the Palestinians. Her spiel took us all the way up to the chorus, where we would burst out, 'Israeli Men! – Hallelujah! Israeli Men! – Amen! Not gonna go out, not gonna let yourself get – shot to shit, It's not Kismet!'

Then there was our version of 'In the Navy', championing the social disability movement, called 'In my Wheelchair'. It featured the line 'In my wheelchair – I put up with lots of stares, in my wheelchair – I want ramps and lifts not stairs...' Great dance routine, making use of a lot of 'loco-motion' style arm pushing movements.

But the finale was my favourite. Everybody loves 'YMCA' anyway, but this one was tailored for the locals. You should have heard us, 'It's fun to stay on the LIE-ON ESS-TATE! Things are so gay on the LIE-ON ESS-STAY-ATE! You're all keeping it real, 'cause you take drugs and steal, and where do you get your next MEE-AALL?'

Offensive? Absolutely. We wanted these guys to be out for our blood. In case you think it was all dancing and pissing about, we were still planning for war. This charade was our one shot at getting them to blow their cover. It was important. Crucial even. It also provided a unique element of surprise. We could taste the moment when we would throw off our sheets and go from wankers to warriors. Can't blame us for getting a bit of enjoyment out of the process. It was a good distraction too. The pre-fight build up can be an energy draining, bowel loosening experience – imagining the worst that could happen, recalling the pain of previous injuries. This gave us something else to think about. On a more personal level, it helped take my mind off Linzi Delaney, Jodie Morgan and Herman McIntyre.

Putting up the posters had given us an opportunity to scout the estate too, so we knew where we were going to stage the performance – right opposite Canvey House, the middle block of the three towers. We'd familiarised ourselves with all entry and exit points, who was covering whose arse, that sort of thing.

Some of us had a weapon of choice, something we could conceal in our robes. There were one or two telescopic batons around, and Tim had a good old-fashioned knuckleduster. Even Kelp had a canister of CS spray that I'd given him for use if any of the action got too close. I was beginning to be impressed with the lad. He'd had hold of it a couple of hours now and he hadn't let it off in his face once.

Plan was, either myself, Geoffrey or Debs would signal if we saw anyone we knew from before. We would front them up and do battle. We would either subdue them or, if they fled, give chase until we caught them. The latter situation had the added bonus of leading us to their lair, with the possibility of finding greater evidence of wrongdoing upon which the police could convict them. We liked the idea of them fleeing. So we planned to be as scary as possible when it all kicked off.

It was either that or incapacitate them with fits of laughter.

The costumes arrived outside in a Ford

Fiesta around 7pm. They were carried in by a woman who looked like Charles Hawtrey with earrings. We couldn't wait to try them on. They were just adapted pillowcases and sheets, but they'd been done really well. They'd taken into account the fuller figures of Nassir and Large Benny, Tim's diminutive stature and, most importantly, they didn't interfere with our dance steps. Sorry, with our ability to ruck, I should say.

I took a step back and surveyed our team.

'Klan. You all look wonderful. Except Tim, of course, who resembles a pint of milk.'

'Fuck off.'

That had me told.

Susie and Freya didn't have the robes. They would just be dressed like, well, like dykes. They would be performing the more intricate bits of dance work in front of the rest of us. We thought that this would have the added effect that all the spectators would see was a bunch of girls – although I think our singing voices could possibly give the game away.

Kelp didn't need one either. Debs and I had decided he was going to sit it out in the van. He hadn't been too happy about this until we told him he would be our soundman. He liked that.

Bic had something to say.

'These guys won't know me, right? It doesn't matter if I don't wear this, right?'

'Ahh, man! You're gonna spoil our look!'

'Trust me, Kelp. I won't. I've got a mate down in Deptford's got a costume that'll fit right in. No problems. I can have it over here by tomorrow morning.'

'OK. Do what you want, Bic. Just don't go embarrassing us. The rest of you okay with the get up?' I asked.

There was much nodding of pillowcases.

'Who's for a pub crawl in full kit?' suggested Debs cheekily.

'I thought that you did not drink, Debra?' queried Geoffrey.

'Gotta have someone sober to save you from getting your asses kicked.'

It was the kind of comment she could get away with.

'Pub crawl – yes. Full kit – no. Don't want to be washing and ironing at nine o'clock tomorrow morning, do we?'

So we headed into town. Despite differing dietary requirements we all managed to stick together and a good time was had by all. We didn't get off our faces because we had a job to do, but this bonding was all still a part of the job. Freya even tried to get

Nassir into a bit of a chat, but he was still finding it really difficult. In the end, she just complemented him on his dancing and he couldn't help but smile at her.

Susie and Freya made a love nest of the Flying Monkey that night. Debs and I contented ourselves with rubbing our sleeping bags up against each other.

Funnily enough, the pair of us had been invited to share the van too. We'd politely declined. I've never had any kind of group sex experience, and I think to leap straight into a mixed race, mixed sexuality, seven-legged, one man foursome, might have been in at the deep end a bit.

Still, would have been something to tell the grandchildren.

28

The next morning we had a quick run through as soon as we got up.

No, it hadn't been a dream. We really could dance. Bic nipped off at around 8.30 and was back by 10 am. He was already wearing his costume when he entered the studio. Instant applause.

He was sporting a brilliant white, sequined, flared jumpsuit. The heavily brylcreemed and quiffed dark hair was his own except for some stuck-on sideburns. He peered at us from behind a large pair of aviator shades before striking an ersatz karate pose.

'That costume is W.A.F,' said Kelp appreciatively.

Bic stared back at him, curled his top lip a little.

'That stands for Wicked As Fuck, man,' he explained.

'Thankyouverymuch...' mumbled Bic, in a rapidly delivered Tennessee drawl.

You had to admit, he set the rest of the Klan off a treat. We went through the routines once more for effect, with Bic as our centrepiece. The line up, from left to right was Nassir, Geoffrey, Tim, Bic, me, Debra and Large Benny. The magnificent bloody seven.

Okay, we weren't magnificent. But we weren't half bad. We sat for a while and discussed rucking strategies, and then we had yet another go at the dancing.

'Come on people, lively up yourself, we're on in an hour,' I shouted to everyone.

'Make up!' shouted Large Benny to no

one in particular. He was really enjoying himself.

Time was indeed ticking towards High Noon. This time we were taking the van with us. It would form a backdrop to our performance and also a means of escape if need be.

One last coffee. One last toilet break. Then Geoffrey Sitcha introduced an eleventh member to our group. His name was Charlie.

Apart from Geoffrey, he only introduced himself to a couple of us – Freya and Nassir as it happens. At last they had something they could share. You could tell Kelp really wanted to meet him too, but I don't think his big sister would have approved.

I've been known to wet my gums on the odd occasion, but I felt like I had an example to set too.

And then we were off down the stairs, out of the door and into the Flying Monkey.

Elvis had now left the building.

29

As the van drew closer to our destination, weaving through potholed streets strewn with the debris of broken homes, we noticed that most of our posters had been torn away.

Good. Someone obviously didn't like us.

Before we even set foot on our concrete stage, out the front of Canvey house, the van was proving somewhat of a novelty in itself. Slack-jawed kids nudged each other then broke into lolloping runs behind us. I don't think they knew why. Perhaps a trace memory of the ice cream vans that might have roamed these streets long ago in more peaceful times.

Debs and I watched out of the back window. Though the kids were running and growing in number, there was no playfulness about them. They were trying their best to look unhurried and disinterested. Don't want to appear uncool. It was like the measured but relentless pace of a hyena pack, wearing down its quarry.

'Weird, innit?' I said to Debs.

'Pied Piper of Tower Hamlets,' she said with a grin.

'Close enough. I hope none of these kids get caught up in it if it all kicks off,' I sighed.

She shrugged and said, 'It's not us starting it. They're not our responsibility.'

I gave a doubtful 'hmmm' before speaking. 'We're knowingly provoking a confrontation.'

'By putting on street theatre? Why shouldn't people be able to express themselves without fear of assault? We're doing nothing wrong.'

She was playing Devil's Advocate. As a couple, we didn't much go in for game playing. But this was an intellectual game rather than an emotional one.

'Debs, some of us are *armed!*'

'I'm not,' she smiled.

'You don't need to be,' I admitted, realising that she had at once taken the moral high ground and reduced the severity of any police charge that may be taken against her. Into the bargain, she hadn't backed down from her position of staunch individualism and had managed to get in a dig about how much harder than me she thought she was. Four–Nil to Debra.

The van rolled to a halt amongst the litter and broken glass of the kerbside. The kids were glad they didn't have to run anymore. Different gangs of slightly older kids, too cool to be seen running, were now sauntering in and began congregating too.

'We're here,' said Tim, rather obviously.

'Let's give it a minute,' I said. 'Build the drama. It's not quite high noon yet...'

It was a couple of minutes to twelve.

We actually had one of those public address systems that they used to use at local elections, with a funnel-shaped speaker on top of the van. At about 30 seconds to go, Kelp switched it on and Strauss's *Zarathrustra*, courtesy of Stanley Kubrick, started building up to a percussive crescendo. All it needed was dry ice. Deep breaths all round and, flinging the back doors open, six hooded and one bequiffed figure spilled out onto the cracked, uneven pavement.

The moment we were out in the open, Kelp segued into the opening piano chords of Robbie Williams' 'Let Me Entertain You,' whilst we all lined up into position.

Freya and Susie stepped out of the driver and passenger doors and came round to the front of the group.

Our audience was growing around us. People who, on a normal day, would probably have steered clear of each other, were standing on the same turf, sharing common ground, to watch a bunch of eejits make arses of themselves and, quite possibly, get a severe slapping.

Perhaps we had struck a blow for unity already.

But there were gaps within the crowd, divisions into subgroups of different ethnic backgrounds, different ages. It was like a prison exercise yard.

The groups of younger kids had a bit of a mixture of race and gender. I dearly hoped that that meant something for the future.

What these people did have in common was that they were poor and angry. The traditional targets for recruitment to fascism. Where hate seethes under the surface of your everyday life, it's easy for someone to come along and harness it. Dress the hate up as hope for a better life. Turn your hate, like a spotlight, on to someone even more vulnerable than yourself – then blame them for how you feel.

The political equivalent of kicking the cat.

In a loud, confident, practised voice, Freya shouted to all who were assembled, 'You are a Community Under Nazi Threat. There are those among you who preach hatred. We are here to sing for freedom and say – don't let these people threaten you … don't let them make a C.U.N.T. out of you!'

At the shouted end of her sentence, Kelp responded. The rolling piano chords blended almost seamlessly into the piano intro for 'Israeli Men' and our first dance number began.

A few people were laughing at us, a few were hurling homophobic invective at us, most just stared like they were watching a motorway pile-up happen in slow motion.

Then I saw Kev. One of Malc's henchmen. He was moving through the crowd in as ghostlike a way as a man of his size was capable. He didn't look well. I don't think it had anything to do with his recent beating. He looked pale. Haunted. He was probably not handling the 'no going back' stress of being a murder suspect on the run.

'Kev,' I said to Debs, nodding in the rough direction, without breaking the stride of my dance steps.

'Eddo too. Someone else with him I don't recognise,' she replied, nodding in the other direction.

By the time we were halfway through 'In My Wheelchair', we had spotted Malc, Russ, and Damian too, dotted around the groups of spectators. Word had gone along the chorus line and we were now all appraised of the whereabouts of the likely suspects. There were at least six or seven other shifty looking characters who, from the way they were skulking about on the peripheries and kept exchanging glances with each other, looked like they were in cahoots. Neither myself, Debs or Geoffrey recognised them from the previous altercation.

Malc had dyed his hair black and combed it forward a little. He now looked like Fred Flintstone. He looked somehow less confident than when I'd last met him. But meaner and angrier and with the same piercing gaze. He stared at us as if he knew that something was not quite right.

But of course there was something not quite right. There was a bunch of queers poncing about and taking the piss in the middle of the Lion Estate. In the middle of their sanctuary. In the place that they hoped even the police couldn't touch them. I hoped that the effrontery and downright bizarreness of it would override their defences. Well, they'd come out for a look, hadn't they?

We'd decided that, if things hadn't come to a head naturally by the end of our final number, Nassir and Large Benny were going to rush Malc and manhandle him into the van – whilst the rest of us warded off any other attackers. We would then make it out of there as fast as the Flying Monkey could carry us, deliver the prime suspect to police custody – thus depriving the rest of the gang of a leader and making any further organised acts on their part less likely.

And, hopefully, we'd all be home in time for tea.

Didn't exactly work out that way though.

As a prelude to our second Village People number, Freya and Susie were doing a little turn of their own while we stood and watched in silence. A more balletic piece, danced to something bassy and ambient by Moby. There was much twisting and lurching and – how can I put it – a somewhat sexual undertone.

Freya was particularly graceful. If you didn't already know she was an amputee, you wouldn't have guessed. She put no weight on her prosthetic limb at any time, but the fluidity of her entire performance made her seem that she was floating on air anyway.

As we stood watching, we all had the sudden feeling that something was about to happen. I noticed one of the shady looking characters who I hadn't recognised before –

a greasy haired little bollix – walking forward and pulling something from his coat. He was too far from us to make any sort of attempt at nailing him.

Shit. I hadn't expected shooters. I never do. I'm just not in that league. When will I grow up?

But it wasn't a gun, though it looked just as lethal.

It was a crossbow. All sleek and curvy and shiny black. Like a handheld Batmobile. Those nearest to him in the crowd scattered away like kicked pebbles.

He raised the weapon to chest height, with a flourish and a smirk. Time slowed as I distinctly heard the click of the trigger above everything else.

The seven inch steel bolt, travelling almost as fast as a bullet, found its victim with a sharp, sick thud and a shattering noise that sounded like more than one bone breaking.

Its victim was Freya.

She'd been a moving target and, although the guy had probably aimed for the centre of her body, it was hard to tell, from one moment to the next, exactly where her body was going to be.

The force of the impact spun her in a most un-balletic way and threw her to the ground. For a brief moment, there was only awkward, twisted stillness where there had been flowing, kinetic grace.

The bolt had speared her shin and had embedded so far that its point could now be seen sticking out of the back of her leg.

Freya sat up slowly with a smile and looked down at her damaged prosthesis.

That girl knew how to work the crowd. She pulled at the bolt with a wince and a grunt, popping it out from the hole in her track bottoms and holding it up.

'Do you want this back?' she asked.

The question was rhetorical. By this time, Tim Marconi had somehow got from his position to the right of me, breezing through the crowd like it was any old Saturday night at Club Zed, and had come up behind the greasy crossbow fella. One polite tap on the shoulder and, as the guy spun round, Tim began some amateur dentistry with the aid of his brass knuckle.

That's when it all went a bit Pete Tong.

The Nazis were momentarily freaked out. First by the lesbian version of the Terminator and now by Casper the Unfriendly Ghost. But, now assessing the threat as one very short but energetic person in a white bed sheet who was, nonetheless, killing one of their crew, they burst collectively into action and rushed Tim from all different directions.

They hadn't twigged that we all came as a package deal. It must have been a hell of a shock when we rushed them, creating one big pavement bundle.

We weren't entirely disorganised though. Large Benny hung back on guard duty, getting Freya and Susie back to the van and keeping them, it and Kelp safe.

Most of the spectators parted like the Red Sea. I bet plenty of them liked a brawl, but only when it was on their own terms. They didn't have a clue what was going on so they just stood back and watched.

We battered into them and hauled Tim out from amongst the flailing bodies, thumping and gouging at whatever was in front of us. Bic broke his thumb trying some fancy Wing Chun arm trapping. I saw Nassir pick a guy off the ground – one hand round his throat and one in his crotch – and throw him a good few feet through the air.

There was probably about a quarter of a second hiatus where we all back-pedalled at the same time and no one was hitting anyone else. In the slow-time of conflict, it seemed to last forever as we looked each other in the eyes.

All told, I reckon there was about twelve of them and only the six of us.

They didn't stand a fucking chance.

30

The element of surprise had been working well for us so far, so we gave it another go.

With each of us yelling as loud as we could, in a move we'd also rehearsed, we threw off our costumes, rushed a few steps forward and stopped, maybe five or six feet away. It was a shock to them and the large group of men flinched backwards as one. Before there was time for any further reaction, Debs and Geoffrey closed the last bit of distance with some legwork. They were our kickers.

Debs spun low with a leg sweep that took her closest opponent to the ground with a thud. Straight up again from the semi-crouch it had left her in, she stomped her heel into the flattened Nazi's groin.

Geoffrey snapped out a low kick to distract the guy nearest to him, quickly chambered the same leg, and shot his foot sideways and upwards into a waiting jawbone – which snapped with a sound like a fat man sitting on a pile of bubble-wrap.

Nassir and Tim burst into action. Little and Large with an attitude, wading into the wall of men. They were more economical in their movements. Fists, elbows, knees, and foreheads – all travelling short distances but handed out with extreme generosity.

Bic was a bit of a concern. His face had gone as white as his Elvis costume. He had been hurt in the scuffle and I think he was beginning to regret his involvement. He could see I was hanging back because of him.

'Get in there, OB. Don't worry about me...'

'Gotta protect the King...' I explained.

'I'll get to the van, send Large Benny in,' he said.

'Okay...'

Just as I was agreeing, a big guy – Russ, I think – swung at me. I managed to duck and give him a dig in the ribs. Unfortunately, the fist I had dodged came swinging towards me again as a backhander. It knocked me sideways.

Luckily, Bic was still there to save my ass. Russ had opened himself up with the swing and Bic was in there with a flurry of chain punches that played the bodybuilder's ribs like a xylophone. He topped it with a *Bil Jee* jab to the eyes. The last move dropped Russ to his knees with a combination of pain, fear and incapacity. But Bic put a final knee to his face just to be safe. He was learning.

Bic grabbed my hand and helped pull me to my feet.

'Can't put muscle on your eyeballs...' he cheerily explained to me, finding his second wind.

'One of my lines,' I reminded him.

Through the throng, my eyes caught Malc's. I could see hatred burning like hot coals. He was seething like a constipated rhino. He looked ready to charge me. But he did a strange thing. He turned and ran.

A strange thing had happened amongst the crowd too. People who had not been involved in the fight had stepped forward. Most of them were black, but not all of them.

These people had formed a solid ring around the Nazis who were out of the fight. I saw Geoffrey hauling a guy by his shoulders and pushing him into the ring of bodies. At that moment, he looked every inch a coked-up badass rather than the son of a well-to-do banker. Anyone who tried to get up and escape was pushed back down.

The captured Nazis were protesting loudly and anxiously. I heard one of the crowd say, 'Tell that to the police...'

I was already running though. Concrete loud with a bouncing echo underfoot. Malc had got quite a head start, was maybe 75 yards in front of me.

I tried to keep the distance. Keep my pace measured and let him tire himself out. I didn't really fancy a one-on-one fight if I caught up with him. He scared me. I'd at least like him to be disadvantaged by being out of breath.

But I noticed that Debs had my back. She was maybe 50 yards behind me. She wasn't breathing hard.

Malc scrambled over a waist-high wooden fence through a succession of sorry looking back gardens, ignoring the vicious barking that his intrusion set off.

I vaulted over the first fence. I was gaining.

Malc could see that the gardens had been a mistake, and I don't mean from a town planning point of view. He veered left and just kicked the last fence over. I was about 40 yards from him now. I could see Debs was in front of us both. Four stories up on a concrete walkway to our left. She was trying to head him off.

How the devil does she do that?

I eased off a bit. I wanted him to keep running. I wanted to see where he went. He didn't disappoint. Turning off suddenly to the right he entered a five-storey block through a side entrance. I could see Debs quickly skid to a halt and double-back to the footbridge she had just passed so she could get over to the same block.

I entered the building and could hear Malc still pounding the stairs, maybe only one floor up from me. I followed as quickly as I could. Three steps at a time. My lungs heaved with the effort but I thanked myself I didn't smoke. I'd have been in a heap outside Canvey House, exhausted from the dancing already.

I could hear Malc; he wasn't as fit as me. The stairs stopped pounding and the slap of boot on concrete lost its echo. He was out of the stairwell and onto one of the floors. I burst through a door and had him in my sight again.

Only for a moment. He disappeared into the doorway of one of the flats and slammed it behind him.

I raced to the door and stopped outside. Debs was about 30 yards ahead of me; climbing over the balcony and onto the walkway I was on. She'd leapt up from a footbridge, one storey below.

'What you doin' here, OB?' she asked. She was maybe a little out of breath.

'Got him,' I pointed at the door.

'Eh? I thought I got a glimpse of him. One story up. Running back the way we came,' she pointed above.

'Can't have been. He didn't have time to get back out.'

'He'd changed clothes too. His hair was different.'

'Nope. Different guy altogether then. No time to change or disguise himself. He's definitely in here,' I said confidently.

Debra shrugged.

'Come to Momma...' she said as she strode towards the door.

We mouthed 'One... Two... Three!' and kicked the door in together. It had an assortment of bolts and deadlocks for security. They all managed to hold but it was a shit door. The frame splintered and the door buckled on its hinges. We dived back in case Malc or any accomplice might be ready to shoot.

Nothing.

We shoulder barged this time, grabbing at the edges of the door as we went, ripping it finally from its hinges and using it as a temporary shield as it swung inwards. We both hit the deck as soon as we were in and rolled for cover. No enemy fire. We leapt back up to our feet. Male was at the back of the room that would have been a living room but was full of boxes and bags.

He was beet red. Wheezing and sweating like a rapist. He had picked up what must have been the first weapon he could lay his hands on. It was a Stanley knife, the old skinhead favourite. I wasn't too impressed.

'More of a visual deterrent than a weapon, Malc,' I chided.

'Are you taking him, or shall I?' asked Debs.

'You don't mind?'

'Not at all.'

I walked towards Malc and kicked him in the balls. He'd barely had time to brandish his knife and now it clattered to the floor as he dropped to his knees. I kicked the knife away from him and then kicked him in the face.

'That's for John,' I said, already unhappy with myself for such a cheap shot.

We looked around whilst Malc lay on the floor and contemplated the next twenty years or so. There were bits of metal pipe and also thick plastic tubing, like drain pipes. There were boxes and boxes of nuts, bolts and nails. There were rolls of twine and thick plastic containers of chemical substances, both solutes and solvents. The guys must have had an account at B&Q.

'If I had to guess,' said Debs, 'I'd say these sorry-ass dipshits were manufacturing nail bombs.'

'That right, Malc? Have we foiled a terrorist plot?'

I was keeping my tone light with bravado but my heart felt heavy. I was sickened by the thought of what such a device could do. But I concentrated on the fact that we had put a stop to this. Right here, right now. As I heard police sirens, I allowed elation to pump in to my heart.

'Let's get him back to the others, Debs. The police won't know where to come looking.'

She picked up a ball of twine and Malc's knife.

'You gonna do some of your Ninja knot-work?'

'Better than walking him in restraint holds all the way back to the van.'

'You're right. Not like he's going to be able to struggle out of your handiwork.'

'I know you know that, OB,' she said with

a smile.

I didn't think the Nazi really needed to hear details of our sex life, but – to be honest – I think he was past listening.

31

Blank-faced residents stood and watched in silent vigil as we led Malc, tied at the elbows and wrists, along the paved walkway that took us back to the three towers at the centre of the Lion Estate. Up ahead, we could see two police vans and three squad cars. Officers in Kevlar vests were milling about in confusion and trying to look busy. For once, no one was throwing bricks at them. The Lion Estate was not a nice, peaceful, law-abiding place, but it seemed that everyone was happy for these particular rotten apples to be removed from the midst of the communal barrel.

Approaching nearer, we could see most of our crew giving statements to notebook-clutching officers. Debra turned to me and said, 'I'll let you take him the last few yards, OB.'

'You don't like the limelight, do you, girl?'

'Police bore me. Questions, questions. Anyway, something's bothering me. I'm going to scout back the way I came.'

And she was gone.

Malc changed his pace a little, like he was thinking about making a getaway.

'Keep walking, Malcolm. There's a good fella,' I said, firmly guiding him by the shoulder.

If looks could kill.

Talking of looks, there was DS Townley up ahead. I guessed most men would jump at the chance of having their particulars taken down by her.

'Little bit off your patch, aren't you?' I asked with a smile.

'I got called out especially 'cause they thought I'd want to be here. Day off 'an all, O'Brien. Can't you restrict your crime fighting to office hours?' She smiled back.

A uniformed officer came over to cuff Malc. He stared in disbelief for a moment at his twine shackles then just shrugged and placed the cuffs on him as well. Malc was led away to one of the waiting vans whilst having his rights explained to him.

'How's it looking?' I asked.

'Like a real result. Everyone we've picked

up has outstanding warrants on them. The crime scene of Pasloe's murder didn't turn up a great deal. I'd say they all wore gloves and they weren't in the business of exchanging any of their bodily fluids. But we're picking up plenty of circumstantial stuff. These guys...' she shook her head, 'they're not rocket scientists.'

'The photos they sent to John's missus?'

'Got it in one. Several partial prints. They must have been passing them round to admire their handiwork before sending them. Didn't put any gloves on. Thought that holding them by the edges would be enough. I think they're all pretty rattled by it now, someone'll fess up or grass up.'

I told her about the address where we'd collared Malc, and all the stuff we'd seen. She looked well pleased. She sent a car straight over and got the place sealed off.

'And what about us?'

'Oh...' She thought for a bit and smiled, 'I'd say you'd all acted with reasonable force given the perceived threat you were presented with. We could do you for not obtaining a council permit for your public performance though.'

'We could appeal to the court of Human Rights that our freedom of expression is being curtailed...'

'Could get messy...'

'Shall we just call it quits?'

'Done.'

'So can we all go home?'

'No. There'll be a few more questions yet, I'm afraid. First question – where's Ray?'

'Ray?'

'Ray "The Lion" Harper. Malc's big brother. This is his manor. Thinks he's untouchable here. He's got to be in on it too.'

'The Lion?'

'It's what people call him,' she shrugged. 'I think he likes it.'

Shit. Val had mentioned this guy before but I'd completely forgotten. That would explain the figure that Debra had seen running away from the flat. The likeness had been niggling her and she'd gone back to check it out.

'I think he's round here somewhere, Val. You lot set to looking for him. I've got to go find Debs.'

Val looked distracted, she was staring past me. Then she said, 'I don't think we'll have to go very far...'

Everything around us hushed and slowed as I turned to see Ray and Debra. They were about 50 yards away from us, on open tarmac, walking slowly to a central position

286

on the parking spaces below Canvey House.

Ray did indeed look a lot like Malc. If anything, he was a little taller, a little broader and his eyes were windows on an even darker soul. His hair was blond like his brother's had been the first night I'd met him. The most important thing about him though, was the screwdriver that he had pressed hard against Debra's throat.

Debs was bleeding from above her right ear, like she'd sustained a blow to the side of the head. Her right arm hung limp like it was broken or nerve damaged. She looked okay – fully conscious and alert – but extremely pissed off to have become a victim. If this Ray dropped his guard for just one moment, I could see she was going to be all over him.

She shot me a quick look, her eyes darting sideways and downward to her right arm then giving me a wink. I took it to mean that her arm wasn't as out of action as she was allowing Ray to believe.

Following the initial hush, officers scattered like balls at the break of a snooker game. Almost instinctively placing themselves between the threat and the public, clearing the deck for the drama to be played out – reducing the variables.

'You have our attention, now please let the

girl go!' A plain clothes officer stood forward and spoke in a loud clear voice that tried to give a mixture of authority, calm and understanding.

'DI Curran,' Val whispered to me. 'He's on call for the local nick this weekend, they were expecting something might happen at the Community Festival tomorrow.'

Ray was grinning a sick grin and shaking his head slowly at Curran's request.

'What do you want, Harper?' asked the detective inspector, the tails of his coat flapping in the spring breeze.

'What do I want?' echoed Ray, in a rasping, 60-a-day voice. 'I want to kill niggers and Pakis and Jews and queers. I want to kill anyone who wants to stop me.'

'That's what you have been doing, Harper. But it's got to stop now,' Curran spoke as if he were merely relaying facts. He now had one hand behind his back, out of Ray's view, and was holding his hand in the position that people make when they're pretending their fingers are a gun. This had not been lost on his colleagues, one of whom was speaking some other sort of code quietly into the RT of the nearest squad car.

'He's putting an Armed Response Unit in place,' Val whispered to me. I think she was trying to be reassuring. I must have gone drip white.

'I'll be taking this bitch with me, whatever happens.' He pressed the screwdriver harder against the soft flesh of Debra's throat. I saw her ears twitch as she tightened her neck muscles, trying to make her flesh less soft. The metal point continued to sink slowly in, though. It looked like Ray would draw blood any second now. But then he seemed to ease off a little. He was enjoying his last stand, milking his blaze of glory for all it was worth.

That little was still not enough for Debs to make any sort of a move though.

Curran repeated his request for her to be set free. As if Ray Harper might somehow relent if he was asked enough times.

At that moment, the speaker on top of the Flying Monkey crackled into life. That was it at first. All the officers looked round at it. Ray did a quick flit with his eyes to see that no one was advancing on him.

Then the brass opening of Edwin Starr's 'War' started up. Not as loud as we'd had it whilst we were doing our dance routine, but just loud enough for everyone to hear.

'Someone turn that bloody music off ... NOW!' barked Curran, his composure beginning to evaporate.

Ray looked suspicious, wise to the tactics of distraction. I don't think he expected the police to look so nonplussed. Debs showed neither surprise nor recognition, but I could see she was bristling with energy – ready for any lapse of concentration on Ray Harper's part.

I had no idea what was going on either but I was about to find out.

With slight movements of his head, Ray did a quick visual all round him. If anyone had been creeping up on him, he'd have seen them. No question. But we sometimes can't see for looking. We are bound by our preconceptions, and there was no way that Ray would have guessed what happened next.

He might have heard something odd, except that the music was masking the motorised whirring behind him.

The next thing we all heard was Ray's screech of agony, as two steel blades – one above the other – plunged deep into his calf muscle.

It was all the opportunity Debs required. She rolled her neck away from the screwdriver, spinning it away in a movement that tore at her skin but went no deeper. Her 'injured' arm awoke with ferocity, glancing elbow first across Ray's temple before wrapping deftly over the back of his neck so that her forearm clamped into his throat. She was now facing in the opposite direction to him.

Jumping into the air, she let herself drop backwards with all her weight plus the added momentum of her leap. Ray was kind enough break her fall with his head. Wrestlers call it a DDT. They rarely do it onto concrete.

The Lion sleeps tonight.

Curran stood there with a look on his face like he was doing long division. Debra just sat there, staring at her mechanical saviour, and said, 'The fuck is *that?*'

Kelp walked forward from his vantage point at the front of Flying Monkey, remote control box in his hand.

'That...' he declared proudly '...is Norman the Nazi Killer.'

32

Seeing as Debs and Geoffrey lived down there, the police allowed them to return for questioning at a mutually convenient time. The rest of us had to get back up to

Yorkshire so we all insisted on getting it over and done with. With plenty of other things for the police to be getting on with, it was early evening before we were all reunited.

We shared picnic tables in front of the nearest pub. The air had a slight chill but we all had the centrally heated feeling of still being totally hyped.

I felt about ten feet tall. God knows how tall Large Benny and Nassir felt. I guess Tim probably felt around six foot.

Kelp, however, was almost literally ten feet tall. He was, without doubt, the man of the match and was rarely off someone or others shoulders. Our metal mascot buzzed around everyone's ankles, delighting children and dogs but scaring the crap out of adults – no knifes though. They'd been removed and handed over to the law.

Nassir and Freya were now thick as thieves. The first thing they'd done when Nassir had arrived at the pub was hug for a good thirty seconds. Screw tradition. We'd faced a dragon together and triumphed. We were more family than family. No matter how much money you make, sex you have and drugs you take, it doesn't get any better than that.

We were in no rush to get back to normal

life. We were staying for the festival tomorrow.

After a night of the best revelry South London had to offer, we marched the next morning under the L.A.B.I.A banner. I have to say we got a few stares from some folks who probably doubted that we were all authentic lesbians. But word soon spread of the exploits of Communities Under Nazi Threat, and before long there were people around us prepared to chant 'We Love C.U.N.T!' as we walked past. Well, I think they were talking about us.

The weather was doing that typical English thing; a bit of everything in moderation. Not too warm, not too dry. A little wet, a little windy – but not enough to moan about.

We watched in awe as Susie and Freya, along with some other friends of theirs, performed their proper piece of street theatre. It made our previous efforts look like the silly game that it had been. Freya must have been taking the piss when she described all street theatre as crap. We cheered ourselves hoarse when they took their final bow. Then we spent the rest of the day cheering at anything else we wanted to.

That evening, we all hugged and kissed and went our separate ways. Tim, Bic, Large

Benny and Nassir headed off to King's Cross. Nassir got a coach back to Manchester; the others got a train all the way to Bradford Forster Square. I'd given Benny a little bit of money to go towards a new van when he got back.

Geoffrey went back to St. John's Wood, telling me to let him know if I ever needed any help in the future.

Susie and Freya and the Flying Monkey motored off to Brighton for a couple of days.

That left me, Debs and Kelp to go back to her place for the night. Kelp, with the aid of Norman, ingratiated himself with the students who lived there and Debs and I tried in vain not to make too much noise.

I got a late morning train the next day. Kelp wanted to stay another day or so. It's not like he had a job to go to.

I didn't exactly have to clock on with anyone, but I felt like there were some matters I should attend to. Herman McIntyre was due another visit. I wanted him to have decided and acted by now. Any part that I was going to play in Jodie Morgan's downfall would depend on how much of the dirty work he left to me.

One thing was for sure. She should know by now that someone had been snooping, and I don't think she needed three guesses who.

I've never been on a train journey, from London to anywhere, where there wasn't a choice of discarded newspapers. I picked up one of the dailies.

It didn't take long before I discovered the small column of news that spoke of a bizarre connection between recent suicides.

I wouldn't be visiting McIntyre after all.

McIntyre was dead.

33

No one came up here now.

He and his wife had used to. Up here was the special place they had come when they were courting. It was where he had proposed and where she had said yes. If, at anytime during their married life, they had had to clear their heads, to cleanse and remember – this was where they came.

Now that was all over. It had been ripped away from him.

He looked out across the Pennine valleys. Up here there was no real horizon. It wasn't as if you could sit and watch the sunset properly. The sun and the moon would fight a battle for the sky each night and each morning. A canvas bearing mixed and swirling colours of changing light above you was a clue to the passage of time. Sometimes the night came before you knew it. Suddenly, you would find yourself tripping myopically as you walked, cursing yourself for being so far away from home.

Tonight, the dark had risen quickly. The moon was full or almost full. He felt like he should know for sure but he didn't. His eyes were blurred with lack of sleep.

The man was naked now.

He'd sometimes idly wondered why the mentally ill were often quick to cast their clothes aside. Maybe he knew now.

He was boiling.

His blood was raging. His skin felt tight and electric, his hair on end – each strand feeling half an inch thick, catching on his clothing until he had ripped it away.

It was anger. Pure bloody anger and rage. Anger at just about everyone.

He tried to remind himself that he wasn't angry with O'Brien. He knew that he had tried to help and to say the right things, but where had it got him?

Nowhere. He was still in this bloody mess.

He knew that, in this state, if he didn't kill himself soon, he'd probably end up killing someone else.

34

I made a few quick phone calls to knowledgeable friends up North. This is what I learnt.

In the early hours of Sunday morning, Herman McIntyre had thrown himself off a railway bridge. The same bridge that Linzi Delaney had thrown herself from two weeks ago.

It was big news in Bradford. The speculation was that McIntyre had been overcome with shame and guilt after the death of one of his patients and had decided to end it all. His wife had commented that, although he had appeared troubled over the past few days, she could not understand why he would have done this. His teenage son and daughter were not available for comment.

There had been no suicide note.

By the time I'd learned enough, my mobile battery was shot, my ear was warm with radiation, I was developing a headache and I was only in Peterborough. I put the phone back in its carry case, sank down in my seat and sighed loudly, getting a couple of looks from fellow passengers.

Did I feel guilty? Had I pushed Herman to do this?

No. I had already worked out my views on suicide over a long period of time and through plenty of indirect experience. Reading the likes of Sartre in philosophy and Durkheim in sociology had given me food for thought. Working with the distressed and downtrodden had given me insights. But what had happened with Linzi had really crystallised it for me.

It was always about choice. It was the last stand of those who felt themselves to be powerless. It was sometimes noble, sometimes cowardly, but always a lone decision. Whatever the pressures that led up to it, the final act always surpassed them. The Self transcending the Other.

I had merely told Herman to do the right thing. This just happened to be his interpretation of it.

So why no note?

The symbolism of jumping from the same bridge was pretty obvious. He wanted people to know there was some sort of connection between himself and Linzi. I knew that the connection was Jodie Morgan. Didn't he want everyone else to know the connection? Was he leaving it up to me after all?

I toyed with the idea that Morgan had killed him. Why would *she* want to make the statement of using the same bridge to make it look like suicide? Was it a message to me that she knew that I knew? It only made sense if I was next on her hit list. She could fucking try.

No. I couldn't see her doing that. She had been blackmailing him. He was a protective shield for the deadly game she called therapy. He was a source of income. She saw him as a weak man. If she was in the business of bumping off her enemies then why not just concentrate on me? If she got me out of the way then she'd have no need to kill Herman. She'd have even more power in his eyes if she could pull that off.

Maybe she was just panicking? Lashing out blindly in a desperate attempt to cover her tracks.

No. I believed it was suicide. But it only made sense if Herman's last stand hit back at his tormentor. Exposing her but without being around himself to bear the pain and humiliation of a spotlight on his activities. There had to be a note. A confession.

Maybe there was. Maybe it just hadn't been found yet. Where would it be? Where would he leave it? Who would he send it to?

Me, of course.

And I just bet that Morgan had come to the same conclusion. Whilst I'd been righting wrongs down South she'd probably been rifling through my home and office. Maybe she had already found what she was looking for.

I did not like the thought of her in my home. I was suddenly worried for the safety of my cat.

The train rattled on like it had all the time in the world. I'd never felt so utterly trapped in all my life.

The quickest way to put my mind at rest was to borrow someone else's mobile. The first guy I asked wasn't going to let me at first, but I slapped a tenner down on his Formica table, grabbed his handset off him and did my best to ignore him.

I breathed a sigh of relief when Mrs. Danvers answered the phone and said the cat was fine. In fact the cat was over at her house and was slightly annoyed at having to get up off her knee so that she could answer the phone to me. She said that there had been no signs of a break-in that she could see. I asked her to nip across the road and check my post and ring me back. She was obliging. The mobile guy was starting to glare at me now.

She called back. I had some mail but, to answer my question, nothing personal looking or hand-written. She said she'd hang onto whatever there was for me.

I phoned the sandwich shop under my office. They'd have known about any break-in because my alarm system is pretty shit hot. They said there hadn't been. The owner knows my code anyway – just in case – so I asked her to pick up any post for me and I'd pick it up from her this afternoon before the shop closed.

Somewhat reassured, I saw no reason not to take the opportunity to order my supper too.

Sorted. Maybe Morgan had been away for the weekend too and hadn't been able to get round to it yet?

I gave the guy his phone back. He sulked at me, telling me that he'd been expecting a call and that I'd prevented him from taking it.

I took a further fiver from my wallet, slapped it down in front of him on top of the tenner that was still there, and told him to have a BLT and a smile and to kindly get out of my face.

When I got into Bradford, about four-ish, I went straight into town and picked up my post from the sandwich shop. I also picked up the pastrami baguette, a bacon and cheddar melt, three packets of crisps and a cranberry juice drink. Thanking them profusely, I headed up the stairs to my office – glancing through my post on the way.

It was there.

An A4 brown envelope containing several different pieces of paper. I quickly saw that some of the pieces of paper were hand-written pleas for forgiveness addressed to his wife and children. I suddenly didn't feel much like reading, so I sat at my desk, switched on the little colour portable and procrastinated.

After eating my sandwiches, watching the *Queen's Nose*, *Newsround* and the early evening news, I finally forced myself to read what was in front of me.

The main body of work had been typed. It was prepared as some kind of formal report. I guessed that maybe that approach had made it easier for McIntyre to face writing about it all. It was rich with detail of meetings between Morgan and McIntyre. It provided evidence of funding that had been made available to her upon her request, and frequent increments in pay unrelated to length of time served or improved performance. There were complaints made against Morgan by both staff and patients that, up until now, had been 'lost'. It argued a strong case for gross misconduct on the part of both of them and criminal activity on the part of Morgan.

He obviously knew that he would not be here to see this report come to light. He spared no blushes when it came to the blackmail. He had even included the photos that I had obtained and details of his meeting with me. He mentioned that I 'acted with honour and integrity'.

I decided not to read his more personal messages to his family. I put them into separate envelopes.

I sat and thought for a while. It was well after dark now. Time to lock up and head to the local nick, just a stroll across Centenary Square. I could have decided to wait and do that in the morning, but I wanted the truth out. It was past mattering for Linzi, Jodie

Morgan could stew for much longer as far as I was concerned, but McIntyre's family had a right to know the truth and I didn't want to keep it from them any longer, even though it would be painful.

The Mental Health service users of Bradford had a right to know too about what had been going on in the name of 'Therapy'. I hoped that it helped rather than hurt to know. I worried that some of them might not be at all surprised.

As I flicked the lights off and turned to head down the darkened stairs, I knew instinctively that there was someone else there. The moment I'd been half expecting. Had Morgan sent someone to silence me? Was a hired assassin crouching in the shadows?

No. As I cautiously leaned round the stairwell, I could see Jodie Morgan herself standing just inside the doorway of the building. This was a gift. She had a smile on her face. I wasn't perturbed. I took it to be a nervous smile.

'So. We meet at last,' I said cockily from the top of the stairs, starting to head slowly down.

She said nothing. The stupid little smirk remained but her eyes narrowed a little.

'Come to bargain with me, have you? Want to split your book collection with me?'

Still silence.

'You're going down, Morgan. See this?' I took the envelope from my pocket and waved it triumphantly, 'Herman's telling on you...'

I reached the bottom of the stairs and got right in her face, waving the envelope in quite an immature fashion. She flinched away from me. The flinch happened at the same time as a sudden movement from my right. Something very solid connected with my skull just above my ear. There was a white flash behind my eyes and I felt instantly nauseous as I collapsed to my knees.

I was still conscious, but I felt like I really, really didn't want to be. Morgan's housemate had been hiding in the little recess at the bottom of the stairs. I looked up to see a serious expression on her face and a double barrel shotgun levelled at me. My hand had tightened around the envelope and it almost ripped as Jodie Morgan swiped it from me. I saw the gun butt swinging back round towards me and only had time to slightly tighten my neck muscles before another explosion made my head swim and dropped me to the floor.

The last thing I felt was cold, scratchy carpet against my cheek. The last thing I saw was a pair of comfortable shoes.

35

When I came round, we were still driving. My senses, particularly my sense of taste, told me it was the Corsa rather than the Merc. Charming. Couldn't even get kidnapped in style. My head was banging like a shit-house door in the wind. The familiar flavour of my own blood in my mouth.

I had been bundled into the back of the car. Can't have been easy, even for the two of them. I'm not exactly built like Kylie Minogue. I had collapsed into the foot-well and cropped hair henchwoman was sitting awkwardly above me, with nowhere to rest her feet. Shotgun pressed against my temple. This will sound odd, but it actually felt good. I was hot and sweaty and the metal was cool. It also felt like it was somehow stopping the pain from getting any worse, stopping my skull from swelling up and bursting, like a cork in champagne bottle.

Morgan was driving. Tight lipped as ever. We carried on in silence. I didn't feel like talking. I know that in those sort of situations you're supposed to create a dialogue with your captors – ram it home that you are a human being with a family, a history. With loves, hopes, dreams and fears. Look them in the eye. Make it harder for them to pull the trigger.

I couldn't be bloody arsed. I bet Morgan would just have got off on it too.

And then we were there. Wherever there was. It was dark. The kind of dark you get up on the moors, away from the sodium lights. The moon was full but was hiding behind grey wisps of cloud like it didn't want to be a witness.

Shotgun Sally could see that I had come round, so she just started jabbing me in the shoulder with her weapon to force me out of the car. I could have refused to budge. Forced them to make a mess of the car when they offed me. But I wanted to see this through to the end. I couldn't believe I'd been suckered so easily and I wanted to redeem myself somehow. Maybe, out in the open, I'd get that chance. Wish my head would pack it in though.

Once I'd half slid and half crawled out onto the muddy, stony ground, I used the car to lean on as I stood up. The surroundings were vaguely familiar. I suppose I've walked or cycled or at least driven over most of the moors in West Yorkshire. But having been whisked away like this, I was having trouble orientating myself.

'Move!' instructed the less silent partner, pushing me between the shoulder blades with the double barrel. I was coming round slowly. A few minutes more and, if that gun made contact with my back again, I would spin round and disarm her. Simple as that.

But for the next couple of hundred yards, they stayed just the right distance behind me as I stumbled up an uneven track of wet mud, rocks and spongy turf. Far enough that I couldn't risk a physical challenge, close enough that I'd be a fool to leg it. At this distance, the dispersed shot would rip me into peppered steak. Morgan held a powerful torch that was trained on me. As I moved, it reflected off puddles of black stagnant water and lit up patches of heather and gorse like random snapshots in a slide show. I stumbled on.

'Stop!' I was told.

For sure, these two had never kissed the

Blarney Stone.

I could make out other shapes now. There were large, rectangular stones, worn with age. Pieces of rusted iron lay in twists and tangles; other pieces hugged the angular rocks – hinting at an industrial application, long since forgotten. I thought it might be an abandoned quarry, but then it came to me. I knew where I was. It was the site of some old mine shafts, up on Penistone hill.

'You figure this is a good place to hide my body?' I asked.

I looked round at them now. Morgan's face was shrouded in darkness behind the light that she held. I could see her partner clearly. There was something close to regret on her face. Was this a chink in her armour?

'I used to come walking here with my husband,' she said, looking right through me. The shotgun did not waver.

'You haven't always been a lesbian then?' I asked. It was all I could think to say.

'He told me that, if anyone fell down one of these old shafts they'd be lost forever.'

'It sounds bad to be lost forever,' I said, not sure where I was going with this. But she was deep in her memories. Not really paying attention. Any second now, I'd make a move.

'He used to make sure I didn't fall. Said he didn't want to lose me like that.'

'You sound lost now. It seems like he wasn't able to protect you after all.' Shuffling on the balls of my feet. Ready to go for it.

There was a very low growling sound. I presumed it was Morgan. I presumed she didn't like the way the conversation was heading. But then there was a rustle in the heather behind her too. The growl came again. Another rustle and then a shape, moving.

Jodie Morgan was just beginning to turn towards the noise when Bill Courtney – stark bollock naked, filthy, hairy, bedraggled and with mad eyes big like saucers – leapt from the undergrowth, knocked her to the ground, and sank his snarling teeth into her throat.

36

Jodie's partner whirled round and screamed in shock, anger or fear. Her finger must have been already tightened around the trigger, I think that's the only reason the gun went off.

The flash came slightly before the noise, momentarily illuminating the bright blood that pumped from Morgan's carotid artery. The loud boom sliced through the screaming and growling. It made my headache seem like a memory. The sound echoed back against the rock and faded to reveal a silence more powerful than anything that had preceded it.

I knew that Morgan and Courtney were dead. Cut to ribbons. They had been too close. The torch Morgan had been carrying had gone, shattered in the blast. There was enough light for me to see the woman still standing, holding the shotgun, now turning to look for me.

I flew at her and decked her. We hit the ground together. The shotgun slipped from her hands and clattered impotently against the rocks. I squeezed her face with my right hand, clamping her cheeks together, ready to punch her with my left. There was no resistance though and I couldn't do it. I was sitting astride her, one fist raised in the air. She was snivelling. Cowering. Quaking with fear. I felt like a bastard. I let my fist drop to my side.

'I was going to hand you the gun...' she told me.

'Sorry,' I said. 'There's only one set of prints on that thing – and they're not mine.'

She wasn't even wearing gloves. I suppose they thought they'd just dump the weapon as well as me.

'My father gave me this gun, after I told him I'd been raped. It was shaking in his hands. It felt so heavy when I took it. He told me to use it if I ever saw the bastard who did it...'

I nodded to let her continue.

'I was scared of it but I took it. Hid it away. When I told Jodie about the gun she said it was a symbol of power, a good thing to have.'

'I doubt she thinks that now.'

She wouldn't look round at where the bodies lay, but she looked me in the face.

'Have I killed them?' she asked.

'I think so.'

Yep, they were dead as deeley boppers.

'Oh my God. What have I done?' She sat up in the mud and just kept repeating the same thing to herself in different forms. She was rocking herself like a child. I sat next to her. After a while I said, 'I'm going to phone the police.'

'Can we have a bit longer? To sit here?'

I didn't see why not.

'A little while. Okay. What's your name?'

'Carla,' she whispered.

'Carla Morgan?'

She did a little shrug. 'Not anymore...'

'Who are you now, Carla?'

I wondered what she was clinging on to right now. Why she was still sitting just feet away from two bloody corpses when we could have been halfway down the hill.

'I'm Carla Courtney.'

'Courtney? Yer man there was called Courtney,' I exclaimed, nodding in the direction of the dead.

'Bill. He was my husband,' she said quietly.

She cried and I held her. I wanted to ask questions but it didn't seem right. After a long time, she stopped crying and I stopped holding her. We walked down the hill until my mobile got a signal. After I'd made the call, we waited in silence. By the time I saw them arriving across the valley, grouse were burbling and pink strands of dawn light were starting to leak upwards into a cobalt blue sky.

37

Sat in an interview room in Keighley police station, drinking shit coffee. All on my own now, my body and mind had frozen in the same position. I stared at the wall. I had caught some flak for the length of time it had taken me before making the call. My eyes had glazed over and my throat had constricted during the reprimand. They'd believed my story though. McIntyre's confession had apparently been found inside the car and I guessed that it went some way towards explaining what I'd been doing up on the moor. Trying to explain my connection to Bill Courtney was a bit of a chore. I had thought about just leaving my previous knowledge of him out of it altogether – but the police tend to spot things like that. In the end, they stopped trying to attach some sinister significance to it. It was just a freaky coincidence. Me, I wasn't so sure. I felt surrounded by death. I thought the world was trying to tell me something.

They'd let me go home soon. There I would snap out of it. There I would drink better coffee.

But I'm not sure I did snap out of it. It took the changing of the seasons to slowly shift me from a melancholy that had descended.

Although good coffee did its bit to help.

Spring had turned to summer. In the cemetery up at Lidgett Green, snowdrops had given way to celandines and forget-me-nots. The grass was lush and long.

I'd managed to get a number for Linzi's uncle who lived in Preston. He'd kindly told me where I could find the grave and pay my respects.

The stone stood out with its newness and its modesty of design amongst the soot-blackened Victorian monoliths. It bore the names of Linzi's parents. The shared date of their death was tragedy enough. An even more recent inscription underneath, referring to their beloved daughter, dated only months later, was one of the bleakest images I've ever seen.

A crow cawed, then flapped past my head in emphasis, settling in a nearby tree to watch me.

I found myself thinking it a small mercy that the list ended there forever. That Linzi had not left someone else all alone in the world without her. All alone, as she had been in her final days.

But really, the list of the dead goes on forever. And we all make the list eventually.

Linzi Delaney was dead.

Jonathon Pasloe was dead.

Herman McIntyre was dead.

William Courtney was dead.

Jodie Morgan was dead.

Right now, someone somewhere would be getting their head kicked in because it was someone else's idea of pleasure to inflict pain. Someone somewhere would be getting blown up, mown down or poisoned by an act of war, terrorism, negligence or ignorance. Someone somewhere would be taking their own life in an attempt to negate the effect of someone else's abuse inflicted upon them.

It would be trite to call it Evil. It's just shit, is all.

And shit happens.

But somewhere, some of us – most of us, I hope – will be doing what we can to shovel it.

I took a deep breath and almost offered up a prayer. But it had been too long since my last confession. Way too long.

Nietzsche famously told us 'God is Dead.'

I knew what he meant. I'd say that Catholic conditioning didn't allow me to truly believe this in my soul, but I thought it was a safe enough bet that God had got so pissed off with us all that he just didn't want to know anymore.

So, no prayer then. But I composed a few lines in my head. Spoke them out loud all the same.

Sing no sad songs, O'Brien
Live life through silent choice
'Cause God's got better things to do
Than listen to your voice.

Couldn't swear to it now, but I think the crow appreciated it.

Acknowledgements

To Christina Rossetti for her poetry.

Love goes out to everyone using or working in mental health services.

Thanks to Mark Timlin for letting O'Brien use the Lion Estate as his playground.

Many thank to the *real* Thamesmead Community Safety Unit for assisting me with my enquiries.

And congratulations to Nick and Gemma

This Large Print Book, for people
who cannot read normal print,
is published under the auspices of

THE ULVERSCROFT FOUNDATION